Sam groaned. "I've got to work with Sanders for a month? Maybe longer?"

"This isn't exactly my idea of paradise, either, Perry," Dallas snapped.

"You just better hold up your end this time," Sam warned her.

"Of all the unmitigated gall," Dallas shot back, her eyes challenging. "You're the one who screwed up last time!"

Lieutenant Brashear chuckled. "This is exactly why I want the two of you to work together on this one. You're the perfect team."

Sam and Dallas both turned to him in bewilderment.

"You're going to be a couple in crisis," Brashear explained. "Two tempestuous lovers being torn apart by unfortunate circumstances. The stress will start to show in noisy fights and tears and bitter recrimination loud enough for the whole neighborhood to hear."

He beamed at his own cleverness. "Like I said, you're the perfect team."

Gina Wilkins has always thought that "pretend marriages" were a great plot device, so adding a "pretend pregnancy" was an even better twist. Part of her inspiration came from the movie *Cactus Flower,* in which Walter Matthau and Ingrid Bergman kept up a pretense of being married and having children—they got so carried away with the charade that they found themselves actually arguing about the children. Gina loved that movie, saying, "It was so much fun!" Which is also what our wonderful Temptation romance novels are all about!

Books by Gina Wilkins

HARLEQUIN TEMPTATION
408—AT LONG LAST LOVE
445—WHEN IT'S RIGHT
459—RAFE'S ISLAND
470—AS LUCK WOULD HAVE IT
486—JUST HER LUCK
501—GOLD AND GLITTER

UNDERCOVER BABY
Gina Wilkins

Harlequin Books

TORONTO • NEW YORK • LONDON
AMSTERDAM • PARIS • SYDNEY • HAMBURG
STOCKHOLM • ATHENS • TOKYO • MILAN
MADRID • WARSAW • BUDAPEST • AUCKLAND

For my editor, Malle Vallik, and senior editor,
Birgit Davis-Todd, who continue to make it a joy for me
to write for Harlequin Temptation.

ISBN 0-373-25621-3

UNDERCOVER BABY

1

IT WAS LATE, after ten in the evening, yet heat still radiated from the pavement beneath Sam Perry's weary feet. He tried to remember the last time it had rained, but failed. He could almost taste the dry dust hanging in the air.

Another August in the South. Why couldn't he have moved up north when his parents had a few years ago to escape the heat?

It hadn't been a good day. Beginning with his aging car's mechanical meltdown, it had gone downhill from there. He'd been hit, yelled at, had coffee spilled on him and had a drunk throw up on his shoes. Some days, it just wasn't worth getting out of bed.

At least he was almost home. His unpretentious apartment building stood in front of him like a safe refuge from the mean streets.

"Hey, honey. Lookin' for a little company?"

A woman leaned against the plain brick wall of his building, barely illuminated by the streetlight half a block away. Through the shadows, he could see riotous blond curls that tumbled around bare shoulders, a black-and-white-striped tank top that molded itself to full breasts, a skintight, black Lycra skirt so short as to almost be unnecessary, and legs that seemed to stretch for a couple of miles before ending in torturous high heels.

Hell, he thought. Did he really have to put up with this crap right outside his own apartment?

"Whatsa matter, sweetie? Cat got your tongue?" Without waiting for an answer, she murmured provocatively, "You're looking kinda lonely, sugar. How about a party?"

Sam felt the weight of his badge and weapon lying heavily beneath his sweat-damp clothing. This wasn't the first time he wished he could ignore them. "Go away. This is a decent neighborhood," he muttered crossly.

She only stepped closer. A soft white hand tipped with long, red nails reached out to stroke his arm beneath the short sleeves of his pullover shirt. "My, aren't you a strong one," she cooed. "We could have ourselves some kinda fun, cupcake. Want to ask me up to your place?"

"I'd rather spend an hour locked in a room with a nest of rattlers," he said and meant it.

Brilliant blue eyes, framed in ridiculously long and thick false lashes, laughed up at him. "Why, sugar. I'm crushed."

Sam had had enough. He was tired, hot and hungry. All he wanted was to lock himself into his apartment, make a sandwich, grab a cold beer and crash in front of the TV for a couple of hours before going to bed— alone. He had just turned thirty. Too damned young to feel this damned old. The realization made him grouchier than usual.

"Knock it off, Sanders," he growled. "Tell me why you're here and then get lost. I'm off duty."

She sighed deeply, then dropped her hand from his arm. When she spoke again, her voice was still husky, but brisk. "Lieutenant Brashear sent a message. He wants to see us both in his office first thing in the morning. Eight o'clock."

"I'm on assignment tomorrow. He knows that."

She shook her head, making her synthetic blond curls dance around her shoulders. "Not anymore. Something big has come up. Looks like we're going to be partners again, Perry."

Sam groaned.

She lifted her chin. "I'm not exactly crazy about the idea, either. Not after you screwed up our last assignment."

"*I* screwed it up? Who's the one—"

"Keep it down, will you?" She glanced around quickly to make sure his outburst hadn't drawn attention. "See what I mean?" she muttered. "You have no self-control. If you hadn't gone crazy during that bust—"

"If I hadn't 'gone crazy,' you'd be dead now," he reminded her bluntly.

"I could have handled it. I *was* handling it, until you charged in like the Lone Ranger on steroids and blew my cover."

"Hell, Sanders, if I'd waited another ten minutes someone would have been zipping you into a body bag and delivering you to your grieving mama. I never expected undying gratitude, but—"

She snorted in a decidedly unladylike manner. "Yeah, right. Who took care of the guy who was about to blow your brains out your ear, hmm?"

"If you'd only—"

She lifted both hands and took a step back from him, farther into the shadows. "Enough. I'm as tired as you are, Perry, and I've still got a couple of hours to pull. You have a problem with this, take it up with Brashear."

"I'll do that."

"Fine." She turned away. Sam figured she had a car stashed somewhere nearby, maybe another cop waiting impatiently behind the wheel.

"Hey, Sanders."

She glanced over her shoulder. "Yeah?"

"You look like a slut."

Her eyes flashed, but her crimson mouth curved into a feline smile. Her voice became liquid seduction again. "I'm paid to look like a slut, Perry. But I think I do it well, don't you?"

She reached out suddenly to shape his right buttock with her palm. And then she squeezed.

Sam jerked away from her, feeling his face warm even as the curse hissed from between his teeth. She'd done it again, damn it. Caught him off guard. "Keep your hands to yourself, Sanders."

Her laugh was victorious. "It'll be tough, but I'm sure I'll manage somehow," she purred. "Sweet dreams, sugar."

Sam glowered after her as she walked away. Well, no. She didn't exactly walk. She undulated. Whether the performance was for his benefit, or a natural result of five-inch stiletto heels, he wasn't sure, but he was male enough to waste a minute or two admiring the motion of that microscopic excuse for a skirt.

It was one hell of a great bod, he thought, feeling the heat of his skin rise a couple of degrees. Too bad Dallas Sanders lived in it.

SAM'S MOOD HADN'T significantly improved by 8:05 the next morning. He'd cut himself shaving, his car was still in the shop, so he'd had to bum a ride to work, and it was already ninety degrees outside. He didn't even want to know the humidity. Probably a hundred and fifty percent.

Lieutenant Brashear was talking on the phone when Sam strolled into his office. A woman sat in one of the two leather chairs arranged on the other side of Brashear's desk. She was reading a report, but glanced up when Sam entered. She had glossy brown hair, cut in a chin-length bob, bright blue eyes and a deceptively soft mouth. She wore a minimum of makeup, which made her look young and natural and wholesome. Her clothing was almost prim—a pale rose blouse beneath a short-sleeved gray jacket that matched a straight, knee-length skirt. Her feet were encased in sensible gray pumps with a two-inch heel. She could have been an office worker or a teacher. Maybe a librarian.

Ten hours earlier she'd been a hooker.

Sam nodded curtly to her. "Sanders," he muttered in greeting.

"Good morning, Sam," she said, her husky voice annoyingly friendly. "Rest well?"

He knew he looked like he'd spent a rough night—which he had. How the hell did she look so fresh and bright-eyed after working until midnight? He ignored her question.

Brashear concluded his call and hung up the phone. "Good morning, Sam."

"Marty. What's going on here? You know how close we are to cracking the Perkins case. Another couple of days and we'll nail the jerk."

Brashear gave what Sam had always considered his life-insurance salesman's smile. Martin Brashear looked like a salesman, actually. Short, thinning brown hair, always neatly trimmed and brushed. Bland, pleasant face hardly marked by the passage of forty-odd years. Kept himself in good shape, always dressed well—Sam had rarely seen him without a tie—kept his shoes polished. Took everything in stride—Sam had sometimes wondered if Marty would lose his composure if a bomb went off two inches from his nose.

"We've got enough on Perkins to pull you off," Brashear assured Sam. "The other guys can wrap it up from here."

Sam hated to leave a job unfinished, but he knew Marty wouldn't pull him without good reason. "What have you got?"

"A possible baby-selling scam down in the west end. Nothing solid, but enough to warrant an investigation. You and Sanders will be on loan to the west precinct. We're figuring it'll take a couple of weeks to establish your cover—another couple of weeks to wrap it up. If all goes well, of course."

Sam groaned. "I've got to work with Sanders for a month? Maybe longer?"

"This isn't exactly my idea of paradise, either, Perry," Dallas snapped.

"You just better hold up your end this time," Sam warned her.

"You can kiss my end," Dallas retorted, her eyes challenging. "Of all the—"

Brashear chuckled. "This is exactly why I want the two of you to work together on this one. You're the perfect team."

Sam and Dallas both turned to him in bewilderment.

"You're going to be a couple in crisis," he explained. "Two tempestuous lovers being torn apart by unfortunate circumstances. The stress will start to show in noisy fights and tears and bitter recriminations loud enough for the whole neighborhood to hear."

He beamed at his own cleverness. "Like I said, you're the perfect team for this one."

Dallas and Sam only glared at each other as Brashear began to elaborate on the assignment.

THEY WERE GIVEN THE weekend to take care of everything that needed doing to clear them for their lengthy assignment. Sam had been told to pack his oldest, blue-collar clothing in pasteboard boxes. Nothing fancy or expensive—which wasn't a problem for him. As often as he went undercover, he had twice as many ragged clothes as suits.

He smiled to himself as he thought of the costume that had been ordered for Dallas. She hadn't been pleased.

Two plainclothes detectives broke into enormous grins the minute they caught sight of Sam on Monday morning. Nick, a short, chubby Irishman, and Walter, a burly African-American, had been partners forever and found special pleasure in the trials and tribulations of their co-workers. They were well-known for their warped senses of humor.

Sam eyed their gleeful expressions with wary curiosity. "Okay, let's have it. What's got you two so happy this morning? Have I been fired and don't know it yet? Someone suing me or charging me with brutality? What?"

Nick widened his pale blue eyes in exaggerated innocence. "Hey, nothing like that, buddy. We just wanted to wish you luck on your new assignment. We think it's going to be real—uh—interesting."

Sam figured they were ragging him about working with Dallas again. Everyone knew Sam and Dallas had had a few problems getting along during the past year, ever since Dallas had first transferred into the department where Sam had worked for seven years.

He sighed. "Okay, have your fun. So I'm working with Sanders. We're both professionals. We can put the past behind us and get the job done."

Walter nodded, his expression much too serious now to be believable. "We're sure you're right, Perry. You and Sanders make a great team."

Nick snickered.

Walter ignored his partner as he asked, "Uh—you seen your partner yet today, Sam?"

"No. I'm supposed to meet her in Brashear's office."

Nick seemed to be overcome with a spasm of what might have been giggles in someone who wasn't a tough police detective.

Walter's dark eyes were gleaming when he said, "She's looking particularly lovely today."

Now Sam knew something was going on. Yeah, okay, Sanders wasn't bad looking—she was damned good-looking, to be honest, especially if you didn't know her as well as Sam did. But they'd all seen her dressed as a hooker, a bag lady, a drugged-out teenager, a prim-and-proper career woman. She must really look interesting today to cause such a stir with these two.

Remembering their assignment, he started to grin. "Where is she?"

Nick and Walter were only too happy to tell him.

"ARE YOU *SURE* I'VE GOT this thing on right?" Dallas fretted, tugging at the front of her cheap flowered top. "It looks weird."

Sergeant Leon Kauffman, the precinct's property supervisor, nodded his balding head enthusiastically. "You have it on exactly right. And it looks perfect. Even more realistic than I'd expected when I first saw it."

"It weighs a ton," Dallas muttered. "And it pinches."

Her best friend, Officer Brenda Pennington, laughed. "I can't get over how funny you look."

Dallas sent her a withering glare. "Thank you so much."

Brenda tossed her long dark hair over her shoulder and grinned. "Just wait until Sam gets a look at you."

Dallas groaned and covered her face with her hands.

From behind his desk, Lieutenant Brashear made a note on an official-looking form, then glanced up at Dallas. "Speaking of Sam, where is he?"

"I haven't seen him yet."

"Sam's always late," Brenda reminded.

"And always grouchy," Dallas added in a mutter.

"If there's nothing else you need from me, I have to take some inventories this morning," Kauffman said.

Brashear waved him out. "If you pass Perry, tell him to get in here. We're waiting for him."

"Yes, sir." Kauffman nodded again and rushed out, typically in a hurry.

Brashear glanced at Brenda. "Is there anything in particular you want, Pennington, or are you just loitering on the job?"

"You know I'm only hanging around to be close to you, Lieutenant," Brenda answered, giving him a melting smile.

He grunted, taking the comment as one of her characteristic wisecracks. Dallas suspected that it was absolutely true. She'd been wondering for several months if Brenda was developing a thing for their boss.

Brenda was thirty-four and single; Brashear, forty-one and widowed for two years. Dallas thought it might be a good match, if they could overcome the awkwardness that would surely result from a personal involvement between them. Not that something like that would stop Brenda, who claimed she was just looking for an excuse to get off the streets and into some man's kitchen. Dallas had scoffed at the words, but Brenda had looked completely serious.

"Haven't you got work to do?" Brashear asked Brenda.

Brenda grinned and shook her dark head. "Uh-uh. Ain't no way I'm leaving this office until Sam has a look at Dallas."

"Go away, Brenda. Catch a criminal or something. Quit harassing your fellow officers," Dallas grumbled. As fond as she was of Brenda, there were times when the other woman could be very annoying. This was one of them.

There was a quick, sharp rap on the door and then it opened before anyone could respond. Sam strolled through, yawning and scratching his unshaven chin. His sandy hair was rumpled and his grubby shirt and jeans as wrinkled as if he'd just crawled out of bed after sleeping in them. "Sorry I'm late. I—"

He stopped, his jaw dropping.

Dallas cringed.

It started slowly. First Sam's hazel eyes crinkled at the corners, digging little furrows into the tanned skin. His firm, usually frowning mouth tilted upward on one side, then the other. The laughter began as a low rumble deep in his chest, and then he held his sides and let it out.

Brashear sighed. Brenda just sat back and enjoyed the show.

Dallas watched the display in a smoldering temper. Damn it, she'd known he would react this way! Why couldn't her costume for this assignment have been a backless leather minidress or a bag lady's smelly rags? Anything but this!

"Laugh it up, Perry," she snapped. "You don't exactly look like a *GQ* model, yourself."

Sam wiped his eyes with the back of one hand. "Oh, man, Sanders, you should see yourself."

"I have seen myself. I look like the Goodyear blimp."

He made a production of slowly circling her, his eyes fixed on the large bulge filling out the front of the cheap and ridiculously ruffled maternity top. And then he chuckled again. "How old are you, Sanders?"

"Twenty-five," she answered warily. "Why?"

"You look like a sixteen-year-old who got knocked up in the back of an old Ford pickup."

Her reply should have singed the five o'clock shadow right off his stubborn jaw.

Brashear interceded, his tone patient. "Knock it off, you two. We have things to go over before you leave. Pennington, go earn your pay."

Brenda pushed herself off the corner of his desk and sketched a snappy, impertinent salute. "Yes, sir." She touched Dallas's shoulder on her way out. "Keep your guard up, Sanders."

Dallas responded to the traditional farewell with the same answer she always gave. "Watch your back, Pennington."

Brashear didn't even wait until the door had closed behind Brenda before going over their cover one final time, making sure Dallas and Sam had their roles straight, their procedures agreed upon. The story was that they were a down-on-their-luck unmarried couple moving into the very low-rent district after having been thrown out of another apartment for failure to pay rent. Sam was to act disgruntled about the imminent arrival of a baby for him to support, making it clear to everyone they encountered that the pregnancy had been an accident, and not a pleasant surprise. His dissatisfaction was to make him surly, and their quarrels were supposed to be noisy and audible to anyone within hearing distance.

Dallas had no doubt that Sam could carry off the role of surly jerk. She just wasn't at all sure about her own part. She was supposed to adore the creep, make it clear to all observers that she would do anything to keep from losing him.

"This is going to be the toughest assignment I've ever had," she complained, shifting awkwardly in the straight-backed leather chair that matched the one Sam occupied. How *did* pregnant women sit comfortably with all this bulk in their laps?

"Don't think you can handle it, Sanders?" Sam asked with a mockingly lifted eyebrow.

"I didn't say I couldn't handle it," she retorted. "I only said it would be tough."

"Neither of you would have been given this assignment if I didn't think you could handle it," Brashear said firmly. "Dallas, it will be up to you to befriend this Polly Jones. She's the one our source named as being the next target for the baby brokers. We need you to get close to her."

Dallas nodded. She had never liked the lies she had to tell when she was undercover, but she was thoroughly committed to her job—whatever reasonable steps she had to take to see her assignments through. If lying would protect an innocent baby from being sold like an unwanted piece of property, then she would lie like a trooper.

Ten minutes later, Brashear seemed satisfied that they had their instructions down. "Good luck," he said by way of dismissal.

Dallas started to stand, was overbalanced by the heavy bulge in her middle, and fell back into the chair. Sam grinned, stuck out a hand and hauled her to her feet. "I can tell right now that this assignment is going to be fun," he predicted.

Dallas had to bite her tongue against a reply that would have strained Lieutenant Brashear's patience a bit more than she was willing to risk.

SAM WASN'T AT ALL SURE the rattletrap of a car they'd been issued would get them to the run-down building in which an apartment had been discreetly scouted out for them. The ripped back seat of the ugly, rusted vehicle was filled with pasteboard boxes and ragged bags. It was supposed to represent everything they owned.

They hadn't said much on the way over. It would have been hard to be heard over the rattling, squeaking and clattering of the car frame, not to mention the wind whistling through the drafty doors and the roar of the unmuffled engine. It was with some relief that Sam turned the key to silence the monster.

Dallas was looking at the dilapidated four-story building with apprehension. Sam wondered for a moment if she was finding the accommodations distasteful. He couldn't blame her, exactly. The building was a slum. Paint grungy and peeling, bricks cracked and crumbling, steps filthy and rickety, bums hanging out on the corners. Still, he'd stayed in worse places during the course of his job, and he knew Dallas had, too. "What's the problem?"

She glanced at him then. "What are we going to do if they don't rent us the apartment? Brashear didn't even mention the possibility."

Sam shrugged. "He didn't think it *was* a possibility. The landlady's not known to be real picky about who she rents to, as long as there's a month's rent in advance. We're supposed to look desperate, remember? In need of a place to live immediately."

Dallas looked from Sam to the building, then back again. She took a deep breath, and nodded. "All right. I'm ready."

Sam thought it was extremely funny that Dallas couldn't get out of the car without assistance.

Dallas didn't laugh.

THE BUILDING'S MANAGER turned out to be a woman in her fifties, artificially red-haired, twenty pounds overweight. There were no smile lines around her discontented mouth. Dallas couldn't help wondering if that was because she had never found anything to smile about. They told her their names were Sam and Dallas Pulaski and that they had lost their lease on another apartment the day before, leaving them homeless. Sam explained that he had enough cash to pay one month's rent in advance, but didn't want to sign a lease.

The landlady, who gave them only the surname Blivens, bought their story quickly enough—particularly when Sam dug into his pocket and pulled out a crumpled wad of bills for the first month's rent. That seemed to suit her just fine in lieu of a lease or rent agreement. Dallas reflected that there weren't exactly prospective tenants lined up at her door. Blivens had already admitted that there were three empty apartments in the fifteen-apartment building, all on the same floor. The third floor, she added, glancing at Dallas's bulging stomach. And there were no elevators.

Dallas swallowed a sigh and earnestly assured the woman that the third floor would be just fine.

The landlady didn't object when they requested to move in immediately. She only shrugged, tucked the rent money into a battered tin box, and tossed Sam a key. "Second apartment on the right," she said. "Don't mess anything up."

"We're not going to be here that long," Sam assured her, his chin cocked at a swaggering angle. "Soon as I get back on my feet money-wise, we're out of here."

"Honey, that's what they all say," Ms. Blivens said in a bored, skeptical tone.

Remembering her own role, Dallas spoke up defensively: "My Sam will get us out of here. Things are kinda tough right now, but as soon as he finds him a new job, us and the baby are going to get a better place. Maybe even a nice trailer park."

Sam threw her a repressive glare. "Shut up, Dallas. This woman don't care about our problems."

Ms. Blivens didn't correct him. Dallas subsided into suitably meek silence, though she couldn't help giving Sam one quick, resentful look. She'd play her part, all right, but there were no rules that said she had to like it!

DALLAS COMPLAINED under her breath each step up the two flights of stairs. By the time she reached the top, she was breathless, sweating and more than ready to shed the bulky harness that added nearly twenty pounds to her weight.

The apartment was every bit as bad as she had expected. A tiny rathole of an eat-in kitchen, so dirty she shuddered to think of eating anything that came out of it. A slightly larger living room that held a ratty couch and two broken-down armchairs along with a coffee table that would probably collapse under the weight of a tea cup. The bedroom was barely large enough to hold the lumpy-looking double bed shoved against one fly-spotted, faded-papered wall, broken-down chest of drawers, and TV tray that served as a nightstand. Dallas couldn't look too closely at the ominous stains on the ripped mattress. The bathroom was as appalling as the kitchen.

Sam made sure the toilet flushed and the shower worked, though he muttered that the water didn't get nearly hot enough to suit him. There was no closet.

They stood in the bedroom, looking around in grim resignation. Dallas eyed the small bed, wondering what the odds were that Sam would volunteer to sleep on the ragged sofa in the other room. She looked at him from beneath her lashes.

He glanced her way at the same time and their gazes held for a moment. Then Sam sighed deeply, ran a hand through his shaggy, sandy hair and managed a rather forced smile. "Hi, honey," he said. "I'm home."

Dallas couldn't hold back a rueful smile.

2

DALLAS'S FIRST PRIORITY after bringing in their possessions was cleaning the apartment. There was no way, she told Sam, that she was living in this dump, even temporarily, without getting rid of some of the filth.

Sam shrugged and told her to "knock herself out." Then he settled as comfortably as possible on the broken-down couch and opened the newspaper he'd brought with him.

The neighbors heard the "Pulaskis'" first noisy quarrel during the next half hour or so. It wasn't staged.

Finally Sam helped with the cleaning, to Dallas's intense satisfaction. It didn't even bother her that he muttered promises of dire retribution the entire time.

"The bathroom's clean," he announced a couple of hours later as he entered the kitchen where she had just finished scouring the formerly grease-caked stove. "Is there anything else you would like me to do? Scrub the walls with a toothbrush, maybe? Repaint? Lay new carpet?"

She ignored his heavy sarcasm. "No, I think that's everything. For now."

He growled.

She straightened and pressed a hand to her aching back. She'd removed the pregnancy harness when they'd started cleaning, but a morning of wearing it combined with two hours of heavy work had left her tired and sore. "I don't know about you, but I'm getting hungry."

"I'm not cooking," Sam said, daring her to challenge him. "Not after scrubbing that disgusting toilet."

She shrugged. "So we'll eat sandwiches. I brought bread and lunch meat."

He nodded. "Okay. That will do."

"We'll split the cooking and housekeeping chores from now on. Fair enough?"

He sighed loudly. "We're working a sting, Sanders, not setting up house."

"We still have to eat and sleep here for at least a few weeks. There's no reason we have to live like pigs just because we're working."

Sam crossed his arms and eyed her mockingly. "I never knew you were so domestic. So how come some lucky man hasn't trapped you in the kitchen with a litter of little darlings around your feet, hmm?"

She glared at him. "I haven't found a man worth putting up with on a permanent basis, that's why. And no one's trapping me in a kitchen!"

"More likely you—"

A knock on the apartment door made them both go still.

Sam glanced down at Dallas's slender figure beneath the voluminous maternity top. "Hide in the bedroom," he ordered, and snatched a beer out of the refrigerator. "I'll get the door."

His sandy hair was mussed, his T-shirt grubby and his jeans ripped at the knees. He hadn't shaved in a couple of days. With the beer in his hand, he looked exactly right for the role he was playing. Dallas sprinted for the bedroom, intending to strap herself into the harness as rapidly as possible in case she needed to make an appearance for whoever was at the door. She didn't like being caught unprepared this way. From now on, maybe she'd better wear the unpleasant contraption all the time.

SAM WAITED UNTIL DALLAS was out of sight before answering the increasingly impatient summons from the hallway. Letting his brows settle into a frown, he jerked open the door. "What is it?" he growled.

His first impressions of the woman in the hallway were of teased black hair, heavily made-up dark eyes, a faint, two-inch-long scar on her right cheek, and the heavy scent of an inexpensive perfume. Only then did he note that she was in the latter stages of pregnancy, a condition emphasized by a too-tight red knit top and black stretch pants.

She tossed her lacquered hair back over one shoulder. "You the guy who owns that heap of brown crap parked in my spot?" she demanded, her Bronx accent sounding strange to his Southern ears.

He lifted an eyebrow. "I didn't know the parking spaces were assigned."

"Everyone knows the spot closest to the trash bin is mine," she said belligerently. "You park in it again and you might just find a few flat tires when you go back to your car."

"Lady, I think you ought to know that I don't like threats."

"And I think *you* ought to know that I ain't no lady," the woman retorted, unintimidated by his tough-guy drawl. "And I got friends around here. *Big* friends, if you get my meaning."

"Sam?" Dallas's tentative interruption made Sam glance around. She was standing in the doorway to the bedroom, her brown hair wispy around her pale, smudged face, her heavy harness back in place beneath the frilly top she wore with maternity jeans. She looked very young and vulnerable and deceptively fragile—and wearily pregnant.

Dallas Sanders was damned good at her job. Even Sam had never even implied otherwise, no matter how she might irritate him in other ways.

"What's going on?" Dallas asked, looking warily from Sam to the woman in the doorway. "What's wrong?"

Sam rolled his eyes. "It's another crazy pregnant woman," he muttered in answer to her question. "Looks like I'm surrounded by them."

Dallas flushed—making Sam wonder how the hell she did that on command—and appeared hurt by his comment, which he knew she wasn't. She looked at their irate caller. "I'm sorry," she said. "He didn't really mean that. He's just tired from moving in. Is there something I can do for you?"

She fell into her part so easily—making excuses for him, looking at him with anxious, adoring eyes. Sam couldn't help but be rather impressed, especially knowing the way she *really* felt about him.

"I was just telling jerko here that I don't want him parking that rusted heap he calls a car in my parking space again. Maybe you can help him remember," the other woman said, chin lifted in cocky bravado, her fists on her hips, enlarged stomach thrust forward. "That is, unless you want my friends to have a little, uh, talk with him," she added.

Dallas's blue eyes widened. "You have friends who would hurt him over this?"

"I got friends who would make him disappear like *that*." The woman snapped her crimson-nailed fingers. "If I asked them to, of course."

Dallas wrung her hands nervously. "We won't park in your place again, will we, honey? We didn't know."

Sam ignored her. He carried his beer to the couch, plopped down on it and picked up the newspaper, which he'd turned to the sports section. He didn't look up from it again.

Appeased by Dallas's intimidated behavior, the other woman relaxed a bit. "Well, now you know."

Dallas stepped closer to the door. "Yes, now we know. We don't want any trouble with our new neighbors. Sam—" She lowered her voice and looked quickly toward the sofa. "Sam's just tired," she murmured again.

A look of what might have been pity crossed the other woman's face. "What's your name, kid?" she asked.

Dallas didn't inform the other woman that she was considerably older than she looked. "It's Dallas," she said. "Dallas Pulaski. And that's my—my husband. Sam."

"Husband, huh?" The other woman obviously didn't believe her—which was exactly what Dallas wanted.

"I'm Polly. I live across the hall. You want to know anything else about the way of doing things around here, you ask me. I guess you could come over for coffee or something sometime if you want," she added, sounding as though she were granting Dallas a great favor.

Dallas suspected that much of Polly's attitude was bluff. She'd seen so many others like her—hiding fear and hopelessness behind anger and aggression. "I'd like that," she said quietly, then looked quickly, timidly over her shoulder toward the sofa. "If it's okay with Sam, of course," she added in a whisper.

Polly rolled her eyes in disgust. "Of course," she said sarcastically. And then she turned to walk away, moving with a sway of hips that might have been sexy had she not been made so awkward by her pregnancy.

"Thank you for stopping by," Dallas said with deliberate inanity, and then closed the door.

"What are you thanking the bitch for?" Sam roared.

Aware of possible curious ears, Dallas yelled back, "Well, you could have said *something!* Do we have to start out making enemies of all our new neighbors?"

"We ain't going to be here long enough to make friends with them," he retorted. "And I don't want you making friends with the likes of her, anyway."

"She seemed nice," Dallas protested, still standing close to the thin, hollow door.

"Nice? She was a dragon lady. And did you get a load of that makeup? She looked like a hooker. Probably is."

"You don't know that!"

"You just stay away from her, you hear?"

Dallas heard a door closing across the hallway. She wondered how much Polly had overheard. Enough, she hoped, to make Polly a bit sympathetic toward her.

The first contact had come sooner than they'd even expected. She just hoped the rest of the assignment worked out as well.

"So what did you think of her?" Sam asked as they sat down to their cold-cut sandwiches a short time later. "Think you're going to be able to get tight with her?"

Dallas was busy trying to figure out how to get close to the table with several pounds of stuffing in her lap. She finally gave up, turned sideways in her chair, and reached for a sandwich. "I think there's a chance," she said. "She looked a bit lonely to me—in need of a friend, maybe. That invitation to have coffee with her sometime was a legitimate one, I think."

Sam smiled. "But she has friends. Big ones, remember?"

Dallas chuckled around a mouthful of wheat bread and smoked turkey. She swallowed. "Did you believe her?"

"Not for a minute."

"Me, neither. But she's got nerve, I'll give her that. You looked pretty tough when you were staring her down at the door, and she never even flinched."

"I looked tough, huh?" Sam seemed to be rather pleased with the description.

Dallas made a face. "Yeah, Mr. Macho. You looked tough. Probably fooled her good."

He lifted both eyebrows, looking a bit offended. "Who was fooling? I *am* tough, Sanders."

"Well, what a coincidence. So am I."

He grinned. She smiled back. And they both blinked, startled by the rare moment of shared humor.

Their visual contact was broken when a raised voice and the sound of shattering glass disturbed them. The noise seemed to be coming from directly over their heads. Both looked automatically upward, as though they could see what was going on above them through the fly-spotted, once-white ceiling.

"Another domestic dispute," Sam commented.

Dallas winced in response to a woman's infuriated shrieking. "Do you think we sounded like that earlier?"

"I hope so," he said with a shrug. "That's what we're supposed to sound like."

She sighed. "Just once it would be nice to go undercover with class. I wouldn't mind being assigned to a ritzy apartment, having a delicious hot meal served by a maid, mingling with the Beautiful People."

She took another bite of cold turkey sandwich and allowed herself to drift for a moment of pleasant fantasy.

Sam cut abruptly into the daydream. "You'd never carry it off."

She straightened defensively. "I would, too."

"Admit it, Sanders, you're blue-collar to your toenails. I bet your dad was a construction worker—a mechanic, maybe," he needled with a grin. "I'm right, aren't I?"

She dropped her gaze to her paper plate, toying with the last quarter of her sandwich. "I don't know," she muttered. "Probably."

"What do you mean, you don't know?"

She scowled at him. "I don't know who my dad was. I don't even remember my mother. She dumped me when I was still in diapers. But I *could* carry off a high-class assignment if I get one. You just wait and see."

"All right, I believe you," Sam conceded, his smile disappearing. "You're good at the job. You probably could carry it off."

Slightly mollified, she drank half a glass of milk, then wiped away the resulting mustache with her fingertips. Their present assignment—unlike the one in her daydream—didn't include napkins. Not even the paper variety.

Sam finished his own meal in silence. He didn't speak again until after he'd tossed the paper plate into a brown paper bag and rinsed his milk glass and set it in the sink. "Dallas?"

She had just cleared away the remains of the meal and was wiping the table with a damp rag. "Yeah?"

"What I said about your father? Well—uh—I'm sorry. I didn't know about—you know—" He cleared his throat, uncharacteristically awkward with the apology.

She frowned and concentrated on her cleaning. She hadn't told him about her background in order to obtain his sympathy. She didn't want sympathy—from Sam or anyone else. She didn't even know *why* she'd told him, since she rarely talked about her childhood. It had just slipped out. "Forget it. No big deal."

She tossed the rag in the sink, wiped her hands on her jeans and spoke a bit too quickly. "So, you think we should have another 'fight' tonight?"

He shook his head. "We don't want to overdo it our first day here." A glimmer of mischief appeared in his hazel eyes. "Why don't we treat the neighbors to some rowdy lovemaking, instead?"

She hated herself for blushing. "I don't think so."

"It would certainly add to our cover," he argued, beginning to smile again. "What do you think, Sanders? Can you fake a noisy orgasm?"

She gave him a withering look. "With you, I'd *have* to—but not tonight. I have a headache."

"Some men might take that as a challenge, you know."

She deliberately turned her back to him. "Give me a break, Perry. I think you've flexed your macho enough for one day. I'm tired. I'm going to bed."

"Just get ready to share it. No way in hell am I sleeping on that couch with its killer springs."

Dallas gave another noisy sigh. "You could always take the floor."

"*You* take the floor if you're so concerned about your virtue."

"I'm not worried about my virtue, Perry. I'm worried about my rest. You probably snore like a buzz saw."

He was caught off guard enough to chuckle. "I don't snore, Sanders. I stayed awake all night once to make sure."

She made a face in response to the old joke, relieved that the issue had been settled with relatively good grace. So she and Sam would be sharing a bed. Big deal. She'd slept in vans, bushes, warehouses, fleabag hotels. All part of the job.

But she'd never slept with Sam Perry. And, for some reason, that seemed quite a different prospect.

DALLAS WORE HER USUAL oversize football jersey for
bed. It was about as sexy as a flour sack—which was
exactly what she'd had in mind when she packed it.
Sam wore a pair of nylon running shorts. Nothing else.
She nearly swallowed her tongue when she first saw
him. Damn. How could she have known he would look
so good without his clothes? Lean, strong, tanned,
sleek.

Great body, she thought, eyeing him surrepti-
tiously. Too bad it belonged to Sam Perry.

Sam looked up when Dallas came out of the bath-
room. He glanced at her nightshirt and curled his lip.
"Something tells me that didn't come from a Victoria's
Secret catalog."

"I'm here to catch bad guys, Perry, not to cater to
your twisted fantasies."

His grin was piratical. "Who said you're in my fantasies, Sanders?"

She tossed her head. "Some things just go without
saying."

He laughed and held up both hands. "All right, let's
call a truce for tonight. I'm too tired to try to outmatch
you."

"You'll never be rested enough for that," she retorted. "But I'll call a truce if you will."

He snapped off the overhead light, leaving the room
illuminated only by the outside lights streaming
through a thin excuse for a curtain over the single window in the room. "Right side or left?"

She blinked, then picked one at random. "Right."

"Fine." He climbed onto the left side of the bed and
settled into the flattened pillow. And then he looked

over his shoulder to where Dallas still stood. "You coming to bed?"

She cleared her throat. "Oh. Yeah, sure."

It took more nerve than she'd expected to make herself walk across the three feet of floor between the bathroom door and the bed and slide under the sheet next to Sam.

Come off it, Sanders. It's only Perry. What's with you tonight? She shook her head in disgust at her own uncharacteristic behavior.

"You got that harness thing handy? In case something comes up in the middle of the night and we have to go out?" Sam asked, already sounding sleepy.

"Yeah. It's on the floor over here. I can get into it quickly if necessary, though I can't imagine why I'd need to in the middle of the night."

"Me neither, but you never know. It's always best to be prepared. In fact," he added, a faint smile in his voice, "maybe you should just sleep in it."

"No way," Dallas said with feeling. "I'd never be able to sleep in that thing."

"Pregnant women do it all the time."

"Yeah, well, I'm just extremely grateful that I'm not really pregnant."

"Think you ever will be?" He sounded only mildly curious.

"I certainly don't foresee it anytime in the near future." For one thing, she thought, it took two to make a baby, and there hadn't been anyone in her life in quite a while. Not since she and Phil split up eighteen months ago because he'd finally realized he detested her job and couldn't continue to be involved with an undercover cop. He'd hated her hours, hated the danger, the seaminess, the dark moods her job sometimes left her in. Had they stayed together much longer, he probably would have ended up hating her.

"What about you?" she asked to distract herself from the painful memories. "You planning a family anytime soon?"

"Hardly. I haven't dated anyone twice since Paula moved out last year," he grumbled into his pillow. "Seems like everyone I meet these days is either a bubble brain or a shrew. Guess the good ones are all taken."

"Oh yeah? And just which of those categories do *I* fit into?"

"I wasn't talking about you, I was talking about the few women I've dated lately. But if I *were* to put you into one of the categories . . ." He left the sentence hanging.

She knew exactly which category he'd place her in. She blew a sharp breath out her nose and rolled onto her side, turning her back to him.

Sam laughed softly, apparently pleased that he'd finally gotten the last word, and settled more comfortably onto his own side of the bed.

Less than ten minutes later he was snoring. Just before sleep claimed her, Dallas made a mental note to give him a hard time about that the next day.

DALLAS WOKE ONLY ONCE during the night. To her dismay, she found herself plastered against Sam's warm, bare back. He was sound asleep, thank heaven, fitted into the curve of her body as though he'd been made to snuggle with her.

She jerked away from him, scooted to the very edge of the bed, and slept fitfully for the remainder of the night, careful not to move inward again.

She didn't even want to *think* about the ragging she'd have gotten from him if he'd awakened to find her cuddled against him like an affectionate kitten.

SAM WAS ALREADY UP when Dallas awoke the next morning. She yawned, stretched, and swung her bare feet over the edge of the bed. The cracked linoleum on the bedroom floor was cool, though the room was warm, since the air conditioner didn't work very well—no surprise. She spent a couple of minutes wondering what color the linoleum was when it was first laid—ten years ago? Twenty?

Finally deciding she was awake enough to be coherent, she stood, ran a hand through her tousled hair, and headed for the bathroom.

Ten minutes later, she wandered into the kitchen, lured by the smell of fresh coffee. Sam was sitting at the spotted chrome-legged table, drinking from a chipped mug and reading a tattered paperback book. He was still wearing the shorts, though he'd donned a white T-shirt with them. Dallas made a determined effort not to look at his long, sturdy bare legs or the gleaming expanse of chest exposed by the V-necked T-shirt as she passed him on her way to the coffee. "Morning," she murmured.

"Where's your harness?" he asked, looking at her slim waist with a frown.

She made a face at him. "Wait until I have my coffee before you start picking on me, will you?"

"I just think you'd better get in the habit of wearing it. You never know—"

"Look, Perry, I know how to go undercover, okay?" she snapped, slamming a cabinet door. Something scurried away from her on the countertop, and she shuddered. "God, I hate this place."

"You haven't even been here twenty-four hours yet. You're really going to hate it by the time this assignment's over."

"Thank you so much for trying to brighten my morning," she muttered, splashing steaming coffee into her mug.

Sam took a deep breath and held up one hand in a conciliatory gesture. "Okay, that's enough. This assignment's bad enough without us sniping at each other."

"I agree. But you started it," she couldn't resist saying as she carried her coffee mug to the table.

He started to speak, bit back the words, then swallowed audibly. "Okay, maybe I did," he conceded. "Sorry."

Her eyebrow lifted. "Was that an apology?"

"Don't push it, Sanders."

She smiled into her mug. "Good coffee," she said a moment later—her own gesture of peacemaking.

He looked satisfied by her effort. "You hungry?"

"What have we got?"

"Chocolate-covered doughnuts or corn flakes." They'd brought in a very limited supply of groceries yesterday.

Dallas shrugged. "Guess I'll have doughnuts. Have you eaten yet?"

"No. I'll have the doughnuts, too."

They both sat without moving for a moment, each waiting for the other to go to the cupboard. Dallas gave in first. After all, she thought, as she set paper plates and the box of doughnuts in front of him, Sam had made the coffee. But he certainly shouldn't get used to being waited on.

"So what's the schedule for today?" she asked, as she slid carefully onto the cracked vinyl seat of the only other chair at the rickety table.

"I'm supposed to start job hunting. I'll ask around, talk to some of the local guys, establish a cover. You might want to go to the corner grocery, meet some of the neighbors."

Dallas nodded. "Maybe I'll ask Polly to recommend a store." It would give her another excuse to get closer to the woman whom their sources had named as the baby brokers' next target.

"Good idea." Sam ate a doughnut in three bites, then reached for another. "Don't forget we aren't supposed to have much money. Can't afford any expensive foods."

She rolled her eyes. "I hate to break this to you, Perry, but I *can't* afford any expensive foods. God knows when I last bought the really good caviar."

He sighed at her sarcasm. "You know what I mean."

"I know what you mean," she agreed coolly. "You're telling me how to establish my cover again—like I don't already know. It isn't necessary."

"Let's not start again."

"I'm not the one who keeps starting it."

Sam scowled and shoved himself away from the table. "I'm going to take a shower."

"Fine."

Dallas sat brooding into her coffee after Sam left the room. It hadn't been a particularly pleasant morning thus far. And she'd been no more agreeable than Sam, she had to admit. Maybe it was because of the unpleasantness of their assignment and their surroundings. Or maybe she was still dealing with the embarrassment of sharing a bed with him. Of course, he really had annoyed her by tossing out instructions as though she were a rather slow rookie desperately in need of his seasoned guidance.

Still, they really should limit their fights as much as possible to the ones they staged for the neighbors' benefit. Whether they liked it or not, they were partners—and partners had to stick together or the results could be disastrous. Even fatal.

Sam apparently reached the same conclusion during his shower. His attitude had improved noticeably when he reappeared, his hair wet, the blue pocket T-shirt he'd donned clinging to damp spots on his back, his legs now hidden by frayed and faded jeans. "You want me to help you make a shopping list before I go out?" he asked.

She shook her head and offered a tentative smile. "I'll just buy whatever's on sale."

He returned the smile. "That'll work." He pulled a ragged hundred-dollar bill out of his wallet and tossed it onto the table. "That should get enough for us to get by on for a few days. It's all we can risk spending at once, I think."

She nodded. "I'll need a few cleaning supplies, too. I used up most of what I brought yesterday."

He started to say something else, then made a face. "I started to tell you to be careful out on those streets alone—but I don't suppose you need me to remind you."

Her smile widened a bit. "No. But thanks, anyway."

"Yeah." He pushed his fingertips into the back pockets of his jeans. "I'll probably be back late this afternoon."

She wondered why she was suddenly reluctant for him to go. And then she decided it was probably only because she knew she was going to be bored to tears in this crummy apartment by herself. She'd just have to find some way to keep herself occupied.

She followed him into the living room, staying back out of view of the hallway when he reached for the doorknob. "Bye," she said.

"That's all the money I've got!" he roared in answer, standing very close to the thin door. "You'll just have to make it be enough."

Dallas didn't even blink at the non sequitur. "But we're out of *everything*," she wailed. "We don't even have milk. The baby needs milk," she added, patting her flat tummy.

Sam jerked open the door, though he held it at an angle that hid her from anyone who might be passing outside. "Look, get off my back, okay? I said that's all I've got. And I don't want to hear anything else about that damned kid today! You got that?"

"But, Sam—"

"Ah, the hell with it. I'm going to try to find a way to make some money. You do whatever you want."

The door slammed behind him as he left.

Dallas smiled to herself, hoping the performance hadn't gone unappreciated. It had been pretty good, actually.

She and Sam might actually pull this thing off.

3

DALLAS HAD SOME difficulty getting herself into the harness that morning. Probably because she was so very reluctant to put it back on, she decided, remembering how quickly she'd donned it yesterday when she'd needed to.

This was definitely one of the more awkward costumes she'd ever worn. The harness was heavy and uncomfortable. Its weight made her back and shoulders ache—even her legs hurt after wearing it for a while. She had to wear a thin, sleeveless T-shirt under it to absorb perspiration and prevent chafing; if only this could have been a winter assignment, she thought with a sigh, fanning her face with her hand as she looked morosely into the spotty mirror.

Even if she *were* pregnant—God forbid—she would never have chosen the limited selection of maternity clothing she'd been given by the department. Most of them looking used, the garments were cheap, flowered, and decorated with so many ruffles and bows that Dallas wanted to gag every time she put one on. She *hated* ruffles! What made maternity-clothing designers think pregnant women with low incomes wanted to dress like the babies they were carrying would be dressed in a few months?

Tugging irritably at the pink-and-white flowered top she wore over pink polyester stretch pants, she turned away from the mirror in disgust and looked for her shoes; then spent fifteen minutes trying to figure out a way to put them on with the bulky harness coming between her and her feet. How *did* pregnant women do these things? And why on earth would anyone deliberately choose to get into this position? And more than once, usually? She shook her head in bewilderment and twisted into an impossible position to tie her sneaker.

Tucking her vinyl handbag under her arm, she stood for a moment at the front door and took a deep breath, willing herself into the role she would be playing for the next few hours. She was well aware that her expression was melancholy and vacuous when she opened the door—just as she intended it to be.

The hallway outside her apartment was dimly lighted and poorly maintained. The once-green paint was dingy and cracked, scrawled with graffiti in places. The light fixtures were rusted; several didn't even work. The flooring was a black-and-dirty-white linoleum of about the same vintage as the floor of her bedroom.

There was a window at each end of the long hallway. The glass hadn't been washed in years. Spiderweb cracks dimmed the sunlight even further. The whole place reeked of cooking odors, among which onion and boiled cabbage seemed prominent at the moment.

Dallas thought sympathetically of the people who had to live here without the comforting knowledge that their occupancy would only be temporary. She'd been in even worse accommodations, of course; seen some places so filthy and disgusting that it had been hard to believe human beings could live that way. It was always children that got to her the most. Someone had to look out for them when their parents failed to do the job—and Dallas had long since appointed herself that task.

She patted her false tummy, thinking of Polly Jones's baby. If Dallas could help it, that helpless infant wouldn't be placed in the hands of people who cared more about cash than human life.

She tapped meekly on the door of Polly's apartment.

"Who is it?" Polly's rather strident voice demanded from within.

"It's Dallas Pulaski," Dallas replied, trying to sound intimidated. "Your new neighbor?"

The door opened.

Polly Jones was not a woman to wear ruffles, even in pregnancy. Her long, bulging body was encased in a tight purple shirt and tighter black slacks, her swollen feet shoved painfully into high-heeled black shoes. Even this early in the morning—barely ten o'clock—her long black hair was already teased and lacquered, her dark eyes heavily made up, her sullen mouth painted a bright red. From appearance alone, Dallas would have judged her to be in her late thirties, but some instinct made her take about ten years off that figure. Polly was probably only three or four years older than Dallas.

"Whaddaya need?" Polly asked, cocking one hip at an angle that looked absolutely painful, considering her condition.

Dallas twisted her fingers in front of her and tried to look shy. "I, uh, have to buy some groceries this morning," she explained. "I thought maybe you could tell me where you get yours. The place with the lowest prices," she added.

Polly shrugged. "Cochran's on the corner of Twenty-third and Polk is probably the cheapest. It's only a couple blocks away, so you can walk if your old man's got the car."

Dallas nodded. "Okay. Thank you."

"They take food stamps."

"Oh, we don't have any food stamps."

Polly looked surprised. "No? How come? Your old man's out of work, isn't he?"

Dallas looked anxious. "Yes, but he's very proud. He won't take assistance."

Polly glanced down at Dallas's protruding middle. "Not even for the kid?"

With a heavy sigh, Dallas shook her head. "He's— he hasn't exactly gotten used to the idea of a baby yet," she said. "He isn't really very happy about it. He says if it wasn't for the baby, we wouldn't be in such bad shape. I'm sure he'll change his mind once the baby gets here," she added hastily, hopefully. "Sam's really a good man. He just worries a lot."

"Ain't that just like a man," Polly muttered in disgust. "Gets you knocked up, then blames you for it. If it was up to me, the whole lot of 'em could just up and die."

Dallas giggled nervously. "I'm sure you don't really mean that."

"Don't bet on it, kid. Hey, you want a cup of coffee? Got some water boiling for instant."

Dallas allowed her face to brighten. "That would be nice," she said, feigning delight that someone—anyone—was being kind to her, as though it were an unusual experience for her.

"Come on in, then." Polly deliberately kept any expression from her own face, but Dallas sensed that the other woman was a bit lonely, herself.

Polly's apartment was laid out exactly the same as the one Dallas and Sam were renting. A small living room, tiny eat-in kitchen, one bedroom and a bath. Like theirs, hers was furnished with cheap, dilapidated, mismatched pieces. There were no pictures on the walls, no knickknacks on display. Except for a slight clutter of discarded shoes and papers and a couple of empty soda cans, the apartment could almost have looked unoccupied.

Leading the way to the kitchen, Polly glanced around as though aware of the impression. "I haven't done any decorating," she said by way of explanation. "I don't plan to stay here long. Just till after this kid's born."

"When is your baby due?"

"About five more weeks." She pressed a hand to the small of her back as she reached for coffee mugs. "None too soon, as far as I'm concerned. I ain't never been this sore and achy in my life. But I guess you know that."

"Uh—yeah. It's not exactly a comfortable condition, is it?" Dallas maneuvered herself carefully into one of the two chairs at the table that was identical to the one in her apartment.

Polly made a face at the understatement. "No," she said wryly. "Not exactly."

She slid a steaming mug in front of Dallas, then took the other seat with her own. "Oh," she said belatedly, after she'd already sat down. "You want sugar or something? I'm out of milk, but I may have some powdered creamer."

Dallas shook her head. "This is fine," she replied, after sipping the too-strong instant coffee. She had long since grown accustomed to lousy coffee.

"So when's your kid due?"

"Not long after yours," Dallas answered vaguely.

"You doing that Lamaze stuff? Not me, I told 'em I want all the drugs they can legally give me."

Dallas chuckled and shook her head. "I'm no masochist," she said. "I'll take advantage of whatever benefits modern medicine can provide." And she would, too, if the time ever came when she had to make that decision, she told herself with a hidden smile.

"Think ol' Sam will go into the delivery room with you?"

Remembering her role, Dallas nodded fervently. "Oh, I'm sure he will. He says he won't now, but I think he'll change his mind when the time comes."

Polly sighed deeply and shook her head. Dallas noted in wonder that the woman's long hair didn't even sway with the movement. *Must be industrial strength hairspray,* she decided, wondering if it would hold up in a windstorm. She almost missed Polly's words: "You really think that guy's going to come around just like that?"

Dallas twisted the coffee mug in her hands. "He'll come around," she insisted. "Sam will be a good father."

Polly shook her head again, and this time there was pity on her face. "Whatever you say, kid."

"Um—what about your baby's father, Polly? Is he helping you now?"

Polly shrugged. "Hell, I don't even know who the father is." She eyed Dallas through her long, heavily-blackened lashes. "Does that shock ya?"

"No, of course not," Dallas said hastily, making sure she looked properly shocked.

Polly laughed without humor. "Yeah, right. Man, where did you come from? A potato farm?"

"Soybeans," Dallas answered, wide-eyed. "My father was a soybean farmer. How did you know?"

Polly laughed again, with genuine amusement this time. Her broad smile erased a good five years from her face. "You really are a piece of work. Hey, you want me to go with you to the store? I can show you around, if you like. And I could use a few things, myself."

"That would be really nice," Dallas said in delight. "Thank you."

Polly gave her a stick-with-me-kid-I'll-take-care-o'-ya look. "You bet."

IT WAS JUST AFTER five-thirty when Sam returned to the apartment. He wiped dust and sweat off his face with the back of his hand, leaving a trail of mud across his cheek. His T-shirt clung wetly to his chest and his jeans were streaked with dirt. The grubby entryway of the apartment building provided little welcome as he wearily entered, but he found himself looking forward to seeing Dallas. Just to find out if she'd learned anything during the day, he assured himself hastily.

An old woman in a faded housedress and sagging knee-high stockings thumped past him behind an aluminum walker. He nodded politely to her and murmured a greeting. She moved closer to the wall opposite him, her pale eyes wary beneath a fringe of straggly gray hair. She didn't return the greeting, and Sam didn't linger. He sensed that she was afraid of him—afraid of everyone, most likely. She'd probably learned her fears the hard way, he thought sympathetically.

Two very young Hispanic-looking children sat in the stairwell outside the second floor, the little boy holding a plastic truck and the little girl clutching a ragged cloth doll. Sam passed them without speaking. He didn't want to encourage them to start talking to strangers, though the darting looks they gave him indicated that they'd been warned about that already. The stairwell was hardly a safe place for them to play, but where else could they go? Out on the streets? He sighed, thinking of the backyard swing set on which he'd spent most of his time at their ages.

The dim third-floor hallway was deserted. He could almost have imagined he was walking through an empty building, had it not been for all the sounds drifting through the thin floor and ceiling—music playing, televisions roaring, a baby crying, a man bellowing someone's name. He thought wistfully of his own apartment building. It wasn't exactly luxurious, but it was considerably more soundproof than this one. And a hell of a lot cleaner, he added with a grimace as he stepped around something on the floor—something he knew he'd be better off not bothering to identify.

He shoved his key into the door of the apartment on the right and let himself in, immediately looking around for his partner. He found her in the kitchen, stirring something in a pan on the stove.

"I hope you're hungry," she said, turning to greet him. "I was starving, so I thought we'd eat early. I— oh," she said, seeing him clearly for the first time. "You're filthy. What have you been up to?"

He couldn't help grinning at her appearance—the ruffled pink shirt and pink pants, the huge bulge of the harness she was still wearing, her hair pulled back into a ridiculously tiny ponytail, her face flushed and damp from the heat of the stove. "I've been working. Who are you pretending to be, June Cleaver? Or Harriet Nelson?"

"Both before my time, Perry," she retorted, then asked, "Working where?"

"Construction crew. A guy walked off the job at lunchtime and the foreman hired me on the spot. I was kinda hoping it would take a few days to find something," he added wearily. "It's too hot for that kind of work."

"Poor baby," she said mockingly. "So, did you talk to any of the guys?"

He shook his head. "Exchanged names with a few, but that was all I had time for today. They kept me running. I'll start talking to some of them tomorrow. I have to report by eight."

She looked at his sweat-drenched clothing. "You'd better keep plenty of water at hand while you're working. You'll dehydrate quickly in this heat."

"The foreman's real insistent on everyone drinking lots of water. He provides it, ice cold. I'll need to pack a lunch tomorrow, though. I never got a chance to eat today."

"Then you *must* be hungry. Go take a quick shower and I'll get this on the table."

"Sounds good. Thanks, Sanders," he said sincerely.

The smile she gave him was surprisingly friendly. "Sure."

Hot water was in short supply in the building, but Sam didn't miss it when he stepped beneath the cool shower. He turned his face gratefully into the spray.

It had been pretty nice coming home to dinner and a smile, he decided, as he reached for the soap. He studied the pink bar for a moment, sniffed it and made a face at the floral scent, then shrugged and began to work up a lather.

It had been almost a year since he'd shared living quarters with a woman. He and Paula had lived together for four whole months after dating for almost a year—a record relationship for him. She'd moved in after assuring him that she would be perfectly happy just to be with him when he wasn't working, that she could accept his long hours and frequently absent nights. Eight weeks later, she'd started complaining.

When she'd started hinting broadly that she had marriage on her mind—and a change of career planned for him—he'd realized that he simply couldn't offer her what she needed from him. When she'd reached the same conclusion, she'd moved out. Last he heard, she was contentedly engaged to an accountant.

The breakup had left him surly and bitter. Not that he'd been deeply in love with Paula; he'd known from the beginning that his feelings for her hadn't been that strong, though he'd been very fond of her. It was just that he'd grown up watching the close, loving relationship between his parents and he'd always vaguely envisioned something similar for himself. He didn't relish the thought of coming home to an empty apartment every evening for the rest of his life—but when it had come right down to it, he'd found himself unable to commit to the one woman who'd made it clear that she wanted marriage and children with him.

He was beginning to believe that there was something lacking in him. Maybe he hadn't gotten a complete set of happiness genes, or whatever the hell it was that made others content with their lot in life. Sam wasn't content. Not with his job, his surroundings, his future—his life. And he didn't know what in hell to do about it.

He shook his dripping head in disgust as he stepped out of the shower. Why the hell was he getting all maudlin now? Dallas was waiting in the kitchen with a fresh-cooked meal and the details of her first day on assignment. He had too much to do to waste time moping over his disappointments.

DALLAS WAS JUST SETTING a casserole dish in the center of the table when Sam rejoined her in the kitchen. She slid her hands out of the tattered oven mitts she'd worn and glanced over her shoulder at him. "You like lasagna?"

"I *love* lasagna," he assured her.

"Good. I know it's kind of hot for such a heavy dish, but I got this sudden craving when I was in the store and saw the lasagna noodles. I hope it's good—I had to buy the cheapest ingredients, of course. There's a tossed salad and whole-kernel corn to go with it."

"Sounds great. What can I do to help?"

"Everything's ready. Have a seat. Oh, do you want iced tea, milk, or soda? I'm afraid the budget doesn't extend to good wine."

Sam chose tea. He was already reaching for the lasagna when he took his seat. "I didn't know you could cook, Sanders."

"There's a lot you don't know about me, Perry," she countered, taking her own seat and reaching for the salad, which she'd served as a side dish rather than a first course.

He realized that her statement was true. He knew almost nothing about her personal life. If she was involved with anyone, he hadn't heard anything about it. He hadn't even known she didn't have a family until she'd let it slip yesterday. She'd been abandoned, she'd said. Had she grown up in foster homes? An orphanage?

It didn't seem quite the time to ask such personal questions. Instead, he settled for teasing. "So, you had a craving for lasagna, huh? Aren't you taking this pregnancy thing a little seriously?"

She wrinkled her nose at him. "Cute, Sam."

He laughed. A moment later he sighed. "Man, this is good. Sanders, I take back a third of the ugly things I've said about you."

"Only a third?"

"I'm feeling generous." He dumped bottled Italian dressing on his salad and stabbed into it with his fork. "So, did you get a chance to talk to our friendly neighborhood hooker today?"

"Polly? Yeah. She made instant coffee for me and went with me to the store. I think she's taking me under her wing. She told the grocer to be nice to me or she'd have her big friends pay him a little visit."

Sam grinned. "How'd you manage that?"

"By convincing her that I was a sweet but slightly dim-witted helpless woman living with a self-centered jerk of a guy who treats her like dirt."

"Me, right?"

"You," she happily confirmed.

He sighed. "And she bought your helpless-little-victim routine? She may be softhearted, but she's not exactly perceptive."

"Hey, I'm good at what I do, Perry. And Polly's sort of nice," she added, stirring her fork through the thick sauce on her plate.

"Nice?" Sam repeated, remembering the loud-voiced woman who'd yelled at him the day before. "Yeah, right."

"She is," Dallas insisted. "She's just had a tough time of it. Her mother threw her out when she was just fourteen because the mother's latest boyfriend was developing a thing for Polly, instead. Like a lot of homeless teenagers, she turned to the streets to support herself."

"And probably a drug habit," Sam added cynically.

"For a time," Dallas said quietly. "She claims she kicked the problem a couple of years ago. She's been trying to save enough money to move somewhere else and start over, but getting pregnant threw her off schedule."

"So how come she didn't have an abortion?"

"Religious convictions. She considers it a sin."

Sam choked on a bite of lettuce and reached for his tea. "You're kidding."

Dallas shrugged. "You should know as well as I do not to try to stereotype people. Some of the most hard-luck cases I've met have often turned out to be more complex than I'd expected. Even Artie Cooper was a devout Catholic, remember?"

Sam scowled at the mention of one of the most ruthless killers he'd ever brought to justice. "So he claimed."

"Nick and Walter said he had a shrine to the Madonna set up in his house. Candles, statue, rosary, the whole bit. His maid said he spent an average of an hour a day there."

Sam shook his head. "This is one hell of a crazy job we're in, Dallas."

"Yeah. But don't you love it?" she asked with a grin.

Sam took another sip of his tea to avoid answering. "Sounds like Polly told you a lot about herself today," he said when he set the glass down.

"She tends to be a talker."

"She say anything about her plans for her baby?"

Dallas shook her head. "The baby was one thing she wouldn't talk about, except to say that she didn't know who was the father. Every time I tried to lead her into a discussion of the baby's future, she changed the subject."

"Sounds like a good indication that she is thinking about selling it."

"Maybe." Dallas frowned and played with her food some more. "But I don't know, Sam. There's something . . ."

"What?" he prodded.

"I don't know," she admitted. "I guess I've got a lot to learn about her yet."

"Yeah, well, don't push it. You don't want to get her suspicious." Almost as soon as the words left his mouth, he realized that he'd unconsciously given her advice on doing her job again. He waited for her to yell at him about it, but she let it pass, surprisingly enough. Since he didn't expect all this goodwill to last, he decided to keep his mouth shut and enjoy it while he could.

SAM DECLARED IT ONLY fair that he clean up the kitchen since Dallas had done the cooking. She didn't argue.

Leaving a spotless kitchen behind him—at least, as much as possible under the circumstances—he rejoined her half an hour later. He found her in the living room, sprawled on the couch, watching a tabloid news show on the portable set he'd brought along with them. The picture was pretty fuzzy, since they weren't connected to cable, but the sound was good. The latest scandal from the entertainment world was being reported in vivid detail.

"I've brought you a soda," Sam said, handing her a canned drink. "If you don't want it, I'll take it back."

She popped the tab. "I want it. Thanks."

"Sure. Shove over, I can't see the TV from the chair."

She made a face, but obediently made room for him on the couch, her movements unusually awkward because of the harness. "I've been tempted all afternoon to take this thing off, but I guess I'd better get used to wearing it."

"Yeah. It has to be uncomfortable," he said, realizing for the first time how bulky and hot the thing must be. "How are you holding up?"

"My back and legs are killing me," she admitted, then smiled faintly. "Polly tells me it's all part of the condition. You wouldn't even want to hear the other distasteful things she complained about."

He laughed. "No, I'm sure I wouldn't. Anything good on the tube tonight?"

She named a couple of popular sitcoms. "That's about it without cable."

He nodded without enthusiasm. "Yeah, okay. Think we ought to have another noisy row tonight?"

She groaned. "I'm too tired to fight tonight. We just had one this morning. Couldn't we wait until you get home from work tomorrow to start another? You can yell at me for not having your food ready or something."

"Yeah, that'll work." He grinned. "Never thought I'd hear you turn down a chance to call me a few choice names."

She shot him a look. "I'll save them up for tomorrow."

As tired as they both were—Sam from his hours of manual labor, Dallas from a day of wearing the harness after a restless night—they were both quiet that evening. It had been a rather pleasant few hours, actually, Dallas realized as the ten o'clock news began. Who'd have thought she and Sam could have gotten along without a real quarrel for an entire evening?

"I don't know about you," Sam said after watching the weathercaster predict another day of blistering temperatures and wilting humidity, "but I'm ready to turn in. Tomorrow's going to be a killer."

Dallas nodded. "Yeah, I'm tired, too."

Sam stood and turned off the TV. Dallas started to rise, then gave an exclamation of disgust when she lost her balance and fell heavily back onto the couch.

Sam laughed, but stuck out a hand to hoist her to her feet. "Sorry," he said. "You gotta admit it's kind of funny."

"I don't have to admit anything of the sort," she grumbled. "You try wearing this thing for a day and see how graceful *you* are."

"I hate to tell you this, Sanders, but I doubt that our cover would hold up long if I was the pregnant one."

"Funny, Perry. Real funny." She pressed her hand to the small of her aching back and groaned.

Dallas changed in the bathroom, donning the same oversize jersey she'd worn the night before. She found Sam in running shorts again, already sitting on the side of the bed and yawning.

It wasn't quite as difficult this time to crawl in beside him—maybe because she'd been mentally preparing herself for it all day.

Sam snapped off the light. "Hot in here," he commented, shoving the sheet off his chest.

"Mmm. Air conditioner doesn't work worth a damn." She stretched out on her side, wincing at the sudden discomfort from a sore spot where the harness had rubbed against her hip. She closed her eyes, hoping a good night's rest would help her find the willpower to strap herself back into the thing in the morning.

"Roll over on your stomach. I'll rub your back for you."

Sam's words brought her eyes open in a hurry. "Uh—"

"Really," he insisted. "You've got to be sore from hauling all that extra weight around. Maybe I can work out a few of the knots."

Dallas thought he might be carrying this good-buddy bit just a tad too far. She wasn't sure she wanted to get that friendly with Sam Perry, for reasons she couldn't have explained at the moment, had she tried. "Thanks, but I know you're tired, too. Get some rest."

But he was already sitting up beside her on the bed, pushing at her shoulder with one hand. "Roll over, Sanders. You can thank me later."

She swallowed a groan and allowed him to shove her onto her stomach. A moment later, the groan escaped when his hands went straight to the small of her back, as though he'd somehow known just where to focus his ministrations. "You're pretty good at this," she had to concede after several long moments in which the only sounds she'd made had been sighs of pleasure.

"So I've been told," he said smugly.

She frowned as she wondered exactly how many times he'd heard the words—and how many women had said them. Not that it was any of her business, of course, she reminded herself hastily.

His hands settled on her shoulders. She winced at his firm kneading of the knotted muscles he discovered there, but a moment later she felt herself turning to oatmeal beneath his palms. He really *was* good at this, she thought. *Wonder if he's this good at . . . ?*

She stiffened. *Whoa, Sanders. Let's not get carried away here.*

"Relax," Sam murmured, pushing his thumbs into the hollows of her shoulders. "You're getting all tense again."

You don't know the half of it, Perry. She cleared her throat and shrugged him off. "That's enough. I feel a lot better now. Thanks."

"You're welcome." He slid back down onto the bed and settled into his pillow with a lot of squirming and shifting. Finally he was still, and Dallas let out a faint sigh. This was much better, she thought firmly. Sam on his side of the bed, her on hers.

Much safer all around.

4

THOUGH USUALLY AN EARLY riser, Dallas didn't wake the next morning until Sam touched her shoulder. She blinked, then squinted up at him, trying to adjust to the light in the room that had been pitch-dark when she'd closed her eyes. Sam was already dressed in jeans and a T-shirt, and he carried a black metal lunch box, looking for all the world like a typical construction worker heading off to the job.

"Sorry to wake you," he said. "But I thought you might want me to let you know I'm leaving."

"Yes, thanks. I can't believe I slept so late."

"It's only seven-thirty. Go back to sleep, if you like. I just wanted you to know you're supposed to be alone in the place—just in case you hear any strange noises from the other room," he added with a smile.

"Oh, thanks so much. I'll sleep just fine now," she grumbled, though they both knew she was teasing. Dallas had long since stopped losing sleep over strange bumps in the night. She'd never sleep at all if she lay awake worrying about that sort of thing.

He ruffled her hair, which was already tousled from the pillow. "See you this afternoon. Don't forget we have a fight scheduled."

"Mmm. I'm looking forward to it," she said around a yawn.

Sam chuckled and took a step backward, then cursed beneath his breath when he nearly fell over Dallas's harness, which was lying close at hand on the floor.

"Hey, watch it!" Dallas said, sitting up and swinging her legs over the side of the bed. "You'll hurt poor Junior."

He grinned, scooped the harness off the floor and tossed it into her lap. "What kind of mother are you, anyway? Leaving your poor unborn child lying on the floor where just anyone could step on it."

Dallas returned the grin, and waved him toward the door. "Get out of here, would you? You're going to be late for work."

His eyes lighted up. "Yeah. Then maybe they'd fire me."

"Forget it, Perry. You've still got to snoop around with the guys there, remember? Baby-selling rumors, right?"

He gave a deep sigh. "Oh, yeah. Right. Have a nice day, Sanders. I want this apartment spotless when I get home, and my dinner waiting on the table."

Her response to him was delivered in a sweet, friendly voice. It was also anatomically impossible, he assured her chidingly as he left for his undercover job.

Dallas realized she was still smiling as she padded into the bathroom after Sam left. She looked at her reflection in the spotty mirror with some surprise, noting that she looked rumpled but oddly pleased with herself, for some reason. Strange. She had almost enjoyed being with Sam Perry the past couple of days.

The heat must be getting to her.

SAM WAS TRYING TO GET enthusiastic about the ham sandwich and apple he'd brought for lunch when he was approached for the first time by anyone wearing what might have been a reasonably friendly expression. He'd soon discovered that high temperatures and closely-supervised, physically demanding work didn't make for a pleasant work environment. His co-workers were too hot and too busy to spend much time sharing pleasantries. So he was a bit surprised when a burly young man in his early twenties approached him at lunchtime with a cold canned soda.

"The boss provides drinks for lunch," he explained. "I wasn't sure if anyone told you."

"Thanks," Sam said, gratefully taking the soda and resisting the temptation to rub the icy aluminum can against his burning face. "I can sure use this."

"Yeah, can't we all." The other man sat on the ground not far from Sam and opened his own lunch box, looking inside without much enthusiasm. "Harding tries to convince us he keeps the drinks iced down out of concern for our morale, but everyone knows he's just trying to keep us from bringing beer in our own coolers. He's a real fanatic about beer on the job."

"Safer that way," Sam agreed.

The younger man shrugged. "A beer or two don't make much difference. Especially in this heat. But I need the job, so I try not to screw up."

"I know what you mean. I wouldn't be doing this if I didn't need the money," Sam said grimly.

"Ain't it the truth." The younger man swept off his yellow hard hat, revealing sweat-soaked red hair. "I'm Jack Reynolds."

"Sam Pulaski."

Jack nodded and stuffed half a sandwich into his mouth. Then he grimaced. "Nothing worse than warm bologna and mayonnaise," he grumbled around a mouthful of bread and meat. "Keep telling my wife to stick to mustard, but she forgets. Or so she claims. Sometimes I think she's gotta be doing it on purpose. Every time she's hacked off with me about something—bologna and mayonnaise."

Sam chuckled. "Women."

"You got a wife, Sam?"

"Sort of." Sam took a bite of his ham sandwich and decided warm mustard wasn't much more appealing than the mayonnaise, though it was probably safer.

"Sort of?"

Sam shrugged. "Got a woman. We've been living together for a while. She sure as hell acts like a wife."

Jack grinned. "It must be genetics or something. Let 'em move in and the next thing you know, you've got a ring in your nose."

"Ain't no ring in this nose," Sam muttered.

"Sure, Pulaski. I hear ya." Still grinning, Jack finished his sandwich and unwrapped a second one.

"Got any kids, Reynolds?" Sam asked after a moment.

"No. Wife's been hinting about having one, but I think we should have a little more money stashed away first. She's going to nursing school. Soon as she finishes, she's going to find a job in a hospital and I'm going to start night classes."

"Yeah? What in?"

"Electronics. You know that business school that's always advertising on TV? They keep talking about how much money you can make repairing computers. I'm thinking about giving that a try. At least it's inside work."

Sam nodded. "Sounds pretty good. Computers are the future, I hear."

"Hell, they've already taken over. And I don't even know how to turn one on. That's why I'm sweating my brains out on jobs a trained monkey could do," Jack complained bitterly. Then he sighed and guzzled half his soda before asking, "You got kids?"

"One on the way."

"Congratulations."

Sam scowled and shook his head. Drops of sweat flew with the movement. "Condolences would be more appropriate. You stick to your guns, you hear? Go to school, get a decent job before you have to support a kid. If not, you'll end up like me, living in a dump with a whining, dissatisfied woman, trying to scrape up enough money for medical bills and baby things."

"Don't want the kid, huh?" Jack asked sympathetically.

"I'd rather have a life," Sam muttered. "Used to have one. Don't know what the hell happened to it."

"Women." Jack shook his head as he repeated Sam's oath.

"Yeah."

"At least you're hanging around," Jack offered, as though trying to find something encouraging to say. "That's more than a lot of guys would do in your shoes.

I know a bunch of guys that split the minute their women got knocked up."

Sam sighed. "It's tempting," he admitted. "Dallas— my woman—well, she's okay. I'd kind of hate to leave her. But this kid—" He stopped and shook his head again, then swiped at the trail of perspiration that trickled down his left cheek. "I just don't know if I'm going to be able to stick it out."

If Jack knew anything about baby sellers operating in the area, it certainly wasn't apparent in his expression. "Hang in there, Pulaski," he said bracingly. "You'll make it somehow."

No, Sam thought. Jack Reynolds wasn't the type who'd lead him to his quarry. Reynolds was still young and optimistic, still of the belief that everything worked out for those who deserved it, that life could turn out just like on TV if one would just be patient. If his wife suddenly announced that she was pregnant—and she probably would before long—Reynolds would simply sigh, mentally bid his lofty plans goodbye and work twice as hard to do what he considered his duty as a man. Poor sap. But Sam almost envied Jack his dreams. At least Jack still had them.

"Hey, Pulaski! Reynolds! You guys planning on getting back to work sometime today? You waiting for a freakin' invitation?"

Sam and Jack exchanged wry glances in response to the bellowed order and closed their lunch boxes. So much for pleasantries.

DALLAS WAS STANDING in the hallway early that evening, chatting with Polly, when she spotted Sam out of the corner of her eye. She turned to greet him with deliberately breathless enthusiasm. "Sam! Hi, honey. You're home earlier than I expected."

He looked without smiling from her to Polly. "What are you doing out here?" he asked, directing the question to Dallas.

"I went out to get your newspaper," Dallas replied, displaying the paper tucked under her arm. "I ran into Polly on the way back in. She was just telling me about—"

"You got my dinner ready?" Sam interrupted, ignoring Polly.

Her bright smile slowly faded. "Well, no, not yet. But it won't take me long to fix something," she assured him hastily, nervously. "I just didn't think you'd be home until—"

"Get inside." Sam's words were curt and cold, his eyes furious.

Dallas privately decided she was glad she knew he was only acting for Polly's benefit. Sam was just a bit too good at this. A meeker woman than she might have been genuinely intimidated by the look he gave her.

Polly moved protectively closer. "Hey, lighten up," she said to Sam. "I'm the one who's kept her out here talking."

Sam pointedly continued to ignore Polly. "Inside, Dallas," he repeated, jerking his chin toward the apartment door.

Dallas swallowed audibly and looked up at Polly. "Don't worry, he'll calm down," she whispered. "He's just hot and tired and—"

"Dallas! Get in the damned apartment!" Sam roared.

She jerked like a startled bunny and scurried toward the door. "I'm coming, Sam. I thought I'd make fried chicken for dinner. You like fried chicken," she said, the words running together in her apparent eagerness to appease him. "And mashed potatoes and gravy. And for dessert we could have—"

The apartment door slammed shut behind them, leaving her and Sam alone in their living room, Polly on the outside. Dallas knew Polly would be listening, so she wasn't surprised when Sam continued yelling at her as though they still had an audience. She threw herself into her own role, loudly defending herself, bursting into noisy wails of distress. She jumped involuntarily when Sam slammed his fist into a wall and ordered her into the kitchen.

She glared at him over her shoulder as she hurried into the other room. He didn't have to look like he was enjoying this quite so much, she thought with a touch of resentment.

She heard the shower running as she set the table and reached into the refrigerator for the cold pasta-and-chicken salad she'd prepared that afternoon. She'd known Sam would be hungry and hot and tired, and would probably want something light but filling. With nothing else to do around the place during the day, it hadn't bothered her to make dinner for him. In fact, she'd spent quite a bit of time on it, telling herself it was the least she could do to uphold her end of the assignment.

She put a basket of crusty rolls and a crock of margarine on the table beside the main dish, along with a bowl of tiny green peas she'd cooked earlier, then reheated in the microwave. By the time Sam joined her, his hair wet and dirty clothes exchanged for shorts and a clean shirt, she was just pouring tea over ice in two large plastic tumblers. "Dinner's ready," she said, nodding toward the table. "Have a seat and dig in."

He looked surprised, then pleased. "Hey, this looks good."

"I didn't think you'd want another heavy meal tonight, as hot as it's been today."

Sam was already filling his plate, and he didn't seem to mind the substitutions in the least. "I'm impressed, Sanders," he said, after taking an appreciative bite of the salad. "It's amazing what you've been able to prepare with a hundred dollars' worth of groceries."

Dallas shrugged, trying to hide her pleasure at the compliment. "I'm used to cooking on a budget. Until I got my promotion last year, I was living on a patrol cop's pay. Before that, I worked two minimum-wage jobs while I put myself through the academy."

He grimaced. "No one ever promised us we'd get rich being honest cops."

"No. But I'm getting by okay now."

"Yeah. Me too, I guess. Of course, it's easier for us— being single," he clarified. "The married guys with families to support complain that they're barely getting by."

Dallas shrugged again. "It's just a matter of knowing how to budget."

He nodded and made a major dent in his dinner before speaking again. "Learn anything new today?"

"Nothing of any importance. You?"

He shook his head. "Nothing. I sure hope Brashear is acting on a reliable tip. I'd hate to think I was going through all this for nothing."

"Does 'all this' include living with me?" Dallas asked politely.

He grinned across the table. "This dinner's got me in such a good mood that living with you seems like a job perk at the moment."

She blinked, then shook her head at him. "Don't get used to it, Perry. The novelty will wear off fast."

"Nothing says I can't enjoy it while it lasts."

"True. But you're cooking all weekend. My generosity only stretches so far."

"So does your shirt," Sam murmured, eyeing the faded blue knit top that was pulled tightly across her bulging middle. "I can't get over how realistic that thing looks, even in a tight shirt."

"It does, doesn't it?" Dallas agreed, glancing downward. "Polly told me today that I look about ready to 'pop.'"

"She's pretty big, herself. When's her kid due?"

"Four or five weeks. She said she saw her doctor this morning and he told her she looks like she'll be on time, if not early."

"Did she seem excited?"

Dallas shook her head, remembering the oddly stark look in the other woman's eyes when she'd talked about her baby. "No. She looked . . . sad."

"She's selling it." Sam sounded convinced.

Dallas didn't know why she was having such a hard time reaching the same conclusion. Maybe it was just because she rather liked Polly, despite her distaste for the life-style Polly had chosen.

Unlike the average armchair liberal, Dallas believed most people did make the choice to become drug addicts and prostitutes or whatever, regardless of their circumstances. She'd known many decent, law-abiding citizens who'd dragged themselves out of horrible backgrounds, which made it difficult for her to accept the badly overused "victim of society" excuse.

Her own past had hardly been a picnic. And it hadn't been a lucky twist of fate that had kept her off the streets. It had been a lot of damned hard work, and a determination to make something of herself, with or without anyone else's assistance. Dallas was a firm believer in the "tough love" philosophy.

Which didn't mean, she assured herself quickly, that she had no compassion. She really did like Polly. If there was anything she could do to help her, she would. But she would also not hesitate to arrest Polly if she did anything illegal with regard to the helpless baby she carried.

Sam pushed his well-cleaned plate away and leaned back in his chair with an exhale of satisfaction. "That was really good, Dallas. Thanks."

"You're welcome."

"Did you get a chance to meet any of the other neighbors today?"

Dallas shook her head. "It's been a quiet day. Of course, with the other two apartments on this floor empty, I don't see anyone unless I go downstairs. I thought I might run into someone when I went out for the paper, but I only saw a couple of little kids playing on the second-floor landing. I saw Ms. Blivens down-stairs and said hello, but she only grunted and kept walking."

"Real ray of sunshine, isn't she?"

Dallas giggled. "Yeah. Right."

"What did Polly tell you about the other tenants? Anything interesting?"

Dallas shrugged. "She talked a little about them yes-terday. Said they're mostly old people on fixed in-comes, too scared to leave their apartments for the most part. Or single mothers on government assistance, struggling to raise too many children without the help of the fathers. Polly's very bitter about men right now. It's obvious that she thinks you're going to dump me to raise the baby alone."

Sam nodded. "That's what we want her to think, isn't it?"

"Yes." Dallas finished her own meal, then reached for her tea. "Sam—you wouldn't do something like that, would you? Walk out on your kid, I mean."

He frowned. "Hell, no, I wouldn't walk out on my kid, if I had one. Even if I couldn't live with the mother, for some reason, I'd make sure my kid was taken care of. Financially, physically, emotionally. I've got no use for those guys who make babies, then disappear."

Pleased with his vehemence, Dallas nodded. "I thought you'd say something like that."

"What about you?" he challenged, turning the ques-tioning back to her. "Can you imagine any circum-stance where you'd sell your own baby for cash?"

"No," Dallas said without even stopping to think about it. "I might not ever get around to having kids, but you can bet if I ever do, nothing would make me sell my child."

Sam searched her face for a moment, then glanced down at her stomach and smiled. "Junior must be really relieved to hear that," he said, lightening the conversation with his teasing.

Dallas went along willingly with the change of mood. She patted her bulging tummy. "I'm getting rather fond of Junior, actually. He's very well behaved. A lot less trouble than most people's kids."

"That's what all the proud mamas say," Sam assured her gravely. "Of course, you realize the kid is half mine."

"Let's just hope he gets my personality instead of yours," she murmured, one hand still resting on the padded harness.

"And my looks," Sam retorted, striking a male-model pose.

Dallas rolled her eyes. "And your modesty, I suppose?"

"Naturally."

She shook her head. "Just as well you and I won't be making any kids together, Perry. Poor little brats would probably get the worst of both of us. Of course, you have a lot more flaws to contribute than I do, but—"

"Hey! I resent that."

"Facts is facts, Perry," she said sweetly.

"Someday, Sanders . . ."

"Yes?"

"Someday," he said firmly, "someone's going to have the last word with you. And I fully intend for it to be me."

"Not in this lifetime, Perry."

He shook his head and shoved himself away from the table. "I'll help you clean the kitchen. Then I might just barely be up to a couple of hours of TV before I crash for the night."

"Real exciting plans," she muttered tongue in cheek, reaching for her plate. "I was hoping you'd take me dancing tonight."

He groaned. "If you knew how many tons of building materials I hauled today, you wouldn't even joke about that."

"You never take me out anymore," she wailed, throwing herself suddenly back into character just to find out what he'd say in return. "I think you're ashamed of me because I'm so fat and ugly."

Sam tossed a wadded-up paper towel at her, but went along with the charade. "Shut up and get out of my way, would you?" he hollered. "How's a guy supposed to relax from a hard day's work with a woman always yapping in his face? Yap, yap, yap—you never give it a rest."

"You don't lo-o-o-ve me!" Dallas complained, her hands busy washing dishes and stacking them in the drainer beside the sink.

"Oh, cripes!" Sam cried in utter disgust. He pulled a canned soda out of the refrigerator and winked at her over his shoulder. "I'm going to watch TV. You sit in here and sulk all night if you want. I don't care."

"Want some cookies to go with that?" Dallas whispered. "Jerk!" she added more loudly.

"Sounds good," he murmured back, then yelled, "Just shut the hell up, all right?"

He stormed toward the living room, popping the top on his soft-drink can as he went. Dallas threw an aluminum pan after him—noisy, but unbreakable. It landed with a satisfying clatter on the linoleum floor, missing Sam by a couple of inches. He gave her a startled look, then shot her a grin before he disappeared.

Smiling, Dallas finished wiping the countertops, then retrieved a handful of Oreo cookies from the cupboard before joining Sam for another quiet evening of fuzzy television.

Fighting with Sam was actually turning out to be rather fun, she'd discovered to her surprise. Lieutenant Brashear had been right about their being well suited to their roles.

SAM WAS STILL ENGROSSED in a news program when Dallas decided to shed "Junior" that evening. She stepped into the bedroom and closed the door, then tugged the maternity shirt over her head and tossed it onto the floor, already reaching for the Velcro fastenings that held the harness on. She sighed in relief when the heavy weight fell away. Setting the apparatus on the floor, she quickly shed her maternity slacks, leaving herself clad only in a white knit tank top and panties. She stretched, shifted her shoulders, then bent double and touched her toes, feeling deliciously slender and unfettered.

The sound of a male throat being cleared behind her brought her upright in a hurry.

Sam was standing in the doorway, an appreciative gleam in his hazel eyes as he eyed her long, bare legs. Aware of the butt-up position she'd been in when he'd entered without her hearing, she blushed and reached hastily for the nightshirt she'd laid out earlier. "I thought you were still watching TV," she said, holding the garment in front of her.

"I'm ready to turn in. Sorry, I thought you'd be dressed. You usually change in the bathroom."

"Yes, well—er—I was just stretching."

"So I saw."

His smirk made her itch to smack him. She lifted her chin and headed for the bathroom, well aware that his attention was still focused primarily below her waist. She closed the bathroom door behind her with a sharp click, then splashed her burning cheeks with cool water. She was already dreading having to cross the bedroom floor and crawl into bed with Sam Perry— especially after the way he'd just looked at her!

SAM LAY ON HIS BACK in the bed, arms crossed behind his head, wondering when Dallas was going to come out of the bathroom. Had she been so embarrassed at being caught in an awkward position that she'd locked herself in for the night? He wouldn't have believed she could be so prudish.

He still remembered exactly how she'd looked when he'd entered the room. Her tanned arms stretched in front of her, her back a graceful curve, her long, bare legs braced to support her. Not to mention that firm, round bottom. He'd always known Dallas Sanders had a great figure. He just hadn't expected to find it displayed quite so appealingly this evening. And now he was going to have to spend another night in bed with her.

He hoped she'd never guess how difficult it had been for him to sleep the past couple of nights. How aware he'd been of her lying so close to him, her breasts rising and falling with her even breathing, her hair tousled against the pillowcase. If she ever found out that he sometimes lay on his side, just watching her and marveling at how young and unguarded she looked in her sleep, she'd probably go for his throat.

The bathroom door finally opened and Dallas stepped out, clad now in another voluminous, unrevealing nightshirt, her eyes carefully avoiding his. She snapped off the overhead light as she passed the switch, throwing the room into deep shadow.

He was rather amused by how careful she was not to touch him as she slid into the bed. She was only an inch or so away from rolling completely off her side of the bed and landing on the floor right next to "Junior."

"I don't bite," he couldn't help telling her, unable to keep the smile out of his voice.

She muttered something incoherent and shifted a quarter of an inch closer.

Directly above them, someone walked heavily across the floor, almost shaking the plastered ceiling above Sam's head. A noisy thud followed, as though that same heavy walker had dropped all his weight onto a bed. A moment later, the bed started to creak, accompanied by a rhythmic thumping sound that might have been a headboard knocking against the wall above them.

Sam had just realized what he was hearing when a woman began to moan. Loudly. A man groaned, then groaned again with more enthusiasm. The X-rated sounds drifted through the thin walls, clearly audible to the unwilling eavesdroppers lying very still in their own bed below.

Dallas murmured a protest and buried her head in her pillow. Sam grinned, then chuckled when the woman above them began to squeal, her words clearly audible for the first time. *"Yes, yes! Oh, God, yes!"*

"Sounds like she's having fun," Sam commented dryly, and shifted to a slightly more comfortable position on the lumpy mattress.

Dallas growled. "Go to sleep, Perry."

"Who could sleep with that going on right above our heads?"

"Try."

The bed above them pounded even more vigorously against the wall. The woman's cries accelerated.

Sam grinned. "Let's just hope they don't drop through the ceiling. I don't want to get quite that actively involved in their personal life."

"Harder! Faster!" the woman shrieked.

Dallas pulled her pillow over her head. "I'm going to sleep," she grumbled, her voice muffled. "Only a pervert would enjoy listening to this."

The woman above them screamed and her lusty lover bellowed. The ensuing silence was startlingly abrupt.

Some ten minutes passed, and Dallas cautiously emerged from beneath the pillow. She sighed in relief. "Thank goodness that's over," she mumbled, turning her back to Sam and squirming a bit to settle back into her usual sleeping position.

Sam tried to ignore her movements. He was uncomfortable enough without thinking about Dallas's temptingly curved bottom wriggling around so close beside him.

He was amused by her reaction to their involuntary voyeurism. He hadn't realized until this assignment that Dallas Sanders was such a conservative type at heart. He never would have guessed by watching her at work in her skimpy hooker clothes and sexy, touch-me-if-you-dare attitude.

"Hey, Sanders?" he said after a moment, giving in to an irresistible temptation.

"Yeah?"

"You've got one hell of a great body."

She went very still, then shrugged against the pillows. "Yours isn't so bad, either. It's what's inside it that I find so annoying."

He chuckled. "Still determined to have that last word, aren't you?"

"Go to sleep, Perry. You've got a long, hard, hot day tomorrow." She sounded suspiciously cheerful about the reminder.

"What?" he retorted. "No good-night kiss? Or maybe we could try to teach the upstairs neighbors a thing or two about noisy lovemaking."

He waited expectantly for an obscene response. What he got was a very chilly reply. "I think not," she said and turned her back more firmly to him. "Good night, Sam."

He smiled up at the now silent ceiling, deciding that her awkward attitude must indicate that she, too, was a bit bothered by their sleeping arrangements. At least she wasn't completely indifferent to him as a man. Now that *would* have been tough on his already battered ego!

5

DALLAS WOKE WHEN SAM did, on Thursday morning. On impulse, she had his breakfast ready and a lunch packed by the time he'd showered and dressed. He didn't question his luck—nor did either of them mention the night before. He returned home dead tired that evening to find dinner on the table again. He thanked her, but was too exhausted to say much of anything else, except to complain that he still hadn't gotten even a hint of a rumor about baby brokers working the neighborhood.

Dallas had to admit that her own investigation wasn't proceeding any more quickly. She'd managed to talk to another neighbor, a homely young woman who lived on the fourth floor with her boyfriend—more likely her pimp, Dallas added matter-of-factly—but no interesting new tidbits had surfaced during that conversation. Like everyone else they'd met so far, the woman hated the building and the neighborhood, and had plans to move out as soon as her finances allowed.

Dallas had noted the ugly scars of old needle marks on the woman's skinny arms, and a fading bruise beneath her heavy layer of makeup. She told Sam fatalistically that she doubted their neighbor would live long enough to move up in the world. He'd looked glum when he'd agreed. He'd turned in soon after dinner, though Dallas stayed up awhile to watch TV.

Sam was sleeping heavily when she joined him in the bed. He didn't even stir. Dallas thought in sympathy that the construction job must really be a killer for someone unused to such demanding physical labor, particularly in the heat they'd been experiencing. She hoped for Sam's sake—and for her own, of course— that the assignment didn't last much longer. Not that they'd made any progress so far.

Dallas had breakfast ready again by the time Sam was dressed on Friday morning. She was just packing his lunch box when he joined her in the kitchen.

"How come you're being so domestic on this assignment?" he asked quizzically, as though he could no longer resist. "Your duties don't really include cooking for me."

Dallas avoided his eyes by industriously scrubbing the skillet in the sink. "I like to cook," she said simply. "I don't get to do it very often. Besides, there's been so little for me to do around here the past few days that it's at least something to keep me busy."

"I never would have dreamed you liked to cook."

"I've warned you before about trying to stereotype me, Perry."

"Yeah. Sorry."

"There are a couple of washing machines and dryers in the basement. Thought I'd do some laundry today. For one thing, it might give me a chance to talk to some of the other tenants."

"Wait until I get home this evening and I'll help you," Sam suggested.

Dallas looked at him with a lifted eyebrow. It wasn't like Sam to fall out of character on an assignment. What was he thinking? "Sam Pulaski wouldn't do laundry," she told him. "That's 'women's work.'"

He grimaced. "Good point. I guess I forgot for a minute." He nodded toward the harness she'd begun to don with her clothing each morning as a means of keeping her own cover firmly established. "There's just something about a pregnant woman that brings out my chivalrous instincts, I suppose."

She made a face. "Gee, and I didn't even know you *had* any chivalrous instincts."

"Sam Pulaski doesn't," he advised her. "Sam Perry's a real prince of a guy."

"Save it for someone who hasn't worked with you before," she advised him. "I haven't forgotten the last job."

"Well, wasn't I trying to save your butt then? Wouldn't you call that chivalrous?"

"I call it stupid. I'm perfectly capable of watching my own butt."

He grinned and let his gaze stroll admiringly from her face to her backside. "Trust me, Sanders. The view's a lot better from this side. Especially in that position you were in when I walked into the bedroom two nights ago."

She gasped and threw a pot holder at him.

He dodged it with a grin and snatched up his lunch box. "Gotta go. I'll be late. Walk me to the door?"

"And why should I?" she demanded.

"Because Dallas Pulaski would," he reminded her logically.

She couldn't argue with that, especially since she'd just lectured him about staying in character. She sighed and waddled reluctantly behind him through the living room.

Sam opened the door, glanced out, then turned and tugged Dallas against him—or as close as possible with "Junior" between them. Surprised, she stiffened, but he covered her mouth with his before she could ask what on earth he was doing.

He kissed her very thoroughly. Very slowly. And after that first startled moment, she found herself so completely lost in the kiss that she couldn't remember why, at first, she'd tried to resist.

There'd been a few times during the past year when Dallas had wondered what it would be like to be kissed by Sam—just idle curiosity, of course, she'd assured herself on the few occasions when the question had crossed her mind. She'd always rather suspected that his kisses would be interesting. But if anyone had suggested that it would only take one kiss from him to turn her into oatmeal, she would have laughed in disbelief.

She wasn't laughing now.

She was breathing rapidly when he finally lifted his head. She stared at him in shock, trying to regain her usual equilibrium. It was marginally gratifying to note that Sam's breathing wasn't quite steady, either, and that his eyes were a bit glazed—just as hers probably were.

All in all, she decided, it was much safer fighting with him than kissing him.

"See you this evening," he told her gruffly. "And you have my dinner ready this time, you hear?"

"Uh—yeah, sure," she murmured, then forced herself to remember the assignment. "I will, honey," she said a bit more clearly. "I'm really sorry about last night. It won't happen again."

"See that it don't," he ordered arrogantly, then closed the door in her face.

It was some time later before Dallas got around to wondering who'd been in the hallway when Sam had first opened the door. She wasn't sure whether she wanted to curse or thank the person for precipitating that kiss.

A TATTERED LAUNDRY basket filled with clothing and supplies tucked under one arm, Dallas peered over the bulge beneath her floral maternity top, trying to watch her feet as she navigated the three flights of stairs down to the basement laundry room. Just guiding herself around was very tricky these days. She was feeling extremely clumsy at the moment. Thank goodness she didn't really have the safety of an infant to worry about on these treacherous stairs! At least if she fell now, she would be the only one injured.

Unless, of course, she landed on top of someone. The thought of Sam Perry sprawled on his smug rear end was quite a satisfying image.

She tried to put Sam out of her mind as she pushed through the cracked peeling door to the laundry room—or at least, she tried to forget about Sam, the enigmatic undercover cop. It was Sam Pulaski, loutish boyfriend and reluctant expectant father, with whom she had to concern herself now.

Ms. Blivens, the surly landlady, was the only one in the room when Dallas entered. The heavy redhead was pushing a mop across the dirty floor without visible enthusiasm—or results. "Don't you go messing this room up," she warned when she saw Dallas. "Got an inspection later this afternoon."

"I won't mess anything up," Dallas promised in her meek, eager-to-please tone. "I just have to wash a few clothes. We're out of clean things."

Blivens nodded, as though regally granting permission. Dallas set the heavy basket on a battered table with a smothered sigh of relief.

"I hear your man got a job working on that new building goin' up on Twenty-first Street."

Rather surprised by her landlady's first attempt at social conversation, Dallas glanced up from the machine in which she was stuffing Sam's filthy jeans. "Yes. He did."

"I also hear you and him don't always get along so good."

Dallas widened her eyes. "Has someone complained?" she asked anxiously. "We didn't mean to disturb anyone. We've had a few quarrels, but they don't mean anything. It's just that Sam gets so tired on his job, he can't help being a little grouchy sometimes."

"Lawd, don't apologize for the guy," Ms. Blivens said in disgust. "He's the one who should be apologizing— yelling at you in your condition. He think it's easy being pregnant?"

"Well, he—"

"It ain't. I should know, I had five kids. All gone now. I'm lucky if I get a card at Christmas," the woman added bitterly.

Dallas didn't quite know what to say, so she kept quiet, hoping the woman would say something of relevance to the investigation. She dropped quarters into the washing machine and held her breath until she heard water gushing into it. From the appearance of the aging machine, she wouldn't have been surprised had it failed to start.

"You been seeing a doctor? You healthy?"

The blunt questions recalled Dallas's attention from the laundry again. She looked over her shoulder. "Yes, I've been seeing the doctor at the free clinic. She said I'm fine, and so is the baby. Thank you for asking," she added, though she wasn't at all sure the questions had been motivated by simple concern for her welfare.

Blivens grunted, then pushed her mop toward the door. "Maybe you and me will be talking again," she said rather obscurely. "I might be able to help you out a bit if you get in any financial trouble."

Dallas kept her expression blandly anxious. "Thank you, but I'm sure we'll be fine. Especially now that Sam's working again. He'll take care of me and the baby. Once we get a little money saved, he'll feel better about everything."

The condescendingly pitying look the landlady gave her reminded her of the way Polly had responded to Dallas's naive optimism. These were women who had long since stopped believing in fairy tales and happy endings; women for whom distrust and pessimism had become second nature. Either one of them would probably be willing to bet much-needed money that Dallas would be raising her baby without the assistance of the father.

Well acquainted herself with men who fathered babies without hanging around to help see them raised— like the man who'd sired her, for that matter—Dallas wasn't surprised by their lack of confidence in Sam. What *did* surprise her was her own certainty that he wouldn't be the kind who "screwed and split," as Polly had put it. Sam had meant every word when he'd said he would personally make sure any child he fathered was provided for.

Funny. She believed him. And like Polly and the embittered Ms. Blivens, Dallas had all too many reasons not to trust any man's words.

"HEY, PULASKI."

In response to the deep bellow, Sam looked over his shoulder as he was walking away from work that afternoon. A group of four men stood together behind him, one of them Jack Reynolds. The one who'd called him, a short, beer-bellied heavy-equipment operator who'd introduced himself as Pete Talley, was mopping at his florid face with a grimy handkerchief. "We're going for a cold beer over at Kelley's," he said, when he saw that he had Sam's attention. "You with us?"

Sam hesitated. "I don't know. My—uh—wife's probably got dinner ready." They had worked almost half an hour late as it was.

Talley snorted. "C'mon, man, it's Friday. Every guy deserves a little break after a tough week. You can call from the bar if you have to report in."

Sam stuck out his chin. "I don't have to report in," he insisted. "I'm just kind of hungry."

Talley shrugged. "They serve sandwiches at the bar. But you do what you want. We're thirsty."

"C'mon, Sam," Jack urged. "Have a couple of drinks with us. Your wife will understand. Mine does. She doesn't like it, but she doesn't gripe about it anymore—much."

"I don't have to answer to my wife," Sam insisted again, allowing himself to sound increasingly defensive.

"Then, come on."

Thinking this might be his best shot at finding out if these guys knew anything about baby brokers in the neighborhood, Sam gave Dallas a mental apology and moved toward the waiting group.

DALLAS SHIFTED INTO A somewhat less uncomfortable position on the couch, turned a page of the newspaper she'd been trying to read, then glanced at her watch. Only ten minutes had passed since the last time she'd checked. It was almost eight o'clock. And the dinner she'd been ready to serve by six was still sitting in the kitchen, cold and increasingly unappetizing.

She reminded herself for perhaps the tenth time that Sam was working. He'd probably found a lead and was chasing it down. She envied him. Anything would beat sitting in this grimy apartment, with twenty bulky pounds of stuffing in her lap and nothing to do but read the newspaper through for the second time or try to watch the fuzzy picture on the TV.

If only she had a book to read. She'd brought a couple of paperbacks, but she'd finished the last one earlier that morning. She'd found plenty of time to read during the past couple of days. Her own part in the investigation was turning out to be increasingly boring and nonproductive.

She'd hoped to talk more to Polly today, or maybe to some of the other tenants. But she hadn't caught even a glimpse of Polly, and the other tenants were still making themselves scarce. Other than that strange conversation with Blivens in the laundry room earlier, Dallas had exchanged less than a dozen words with anyone all day. No one had done any laundry while she was washing—didn't anyone in this building wear clean clothing?—and the two people she'd passed in the hallway had responded to her cheery greeting with wary looks of suspicion.

What ever happened to old Southern friendliness? she asked herself, thoroughly disgruntled. Used to be that everyone greeted everyone. Smiles, waves, nods— even to strangers.

But things had changed, she thought sadly, even in the South. Especially in the poverty-stricken neighborhoods of large Southern cities decimated by crime and drugs and government neglect. No wonder the other hapless tenants of this gloomy residence had learned to distrust everyone who approached them with a snake-oil salesman's smile.

She ran a hand through her brown hair, noting absently that it needed to be trimmed and styled. She hadn't been styling it much during the past week— simply washing it and letting it dry straight and limp, rather than curling it into the sleek curve she favored when she wasn't undercover. And she'd switched from her usual tastefully understated makeup to the brighter colors normally associated with less expensive brands—rosy blusher, blue eye-shadow, bright pink lipstick. Not to mention the cheap, frilly, tent-size garments she'd been forced to wear.

Her appearance usually didn't bother her when she was working on an assignment. There'd been times when she'd been so filthy and bedraggled she hardly recognized herself in the mirror. So why was she fretting about it this time?

She looked at her watch again and cursed under her breath at the realization that only five minutes had crawled by since the last time. Where the hell was Sam?

He really should have told her he would be late, she thought sullenly.

"C'MON, SAM, HAVE another beer. It's still early yet."

Sprawled in a too-small bar chair, Sam tried to focus on his watch. "I don't know," he said. "I'd probably better get on home."

"That woman really does lead you around by the short hairs, don't she, Pulaski?" Pete Talley asked mockingly, his small eyes glassy from the number of drinks he'd tossed down in the past couple of hours.

Sam thrust out his chin. "Hell, no. I wasn't going home because of what she might say."

"So how come you're leaving?" Talley prodded. "Ain't you having a good time?"

"Maybe you had better go on home, Sam," young Jack Reynolds interceded. He looked at Talley as he explained, "Sam's wife is pregnant. It's probably not good for her to get mad at him."

Sam snorted. "Then she's already in trouble. She *stays* mad at me," he said with feeling.

"Pregnant women," a thin, balding man by the name of R. J. Brewer groaned. "They're crazy, I tell you. Both times my wife was pregnant I thought I was going to have to lock her up somewhere. Cried all the time, whined about every little thing, ate like Godzilla." He shook his shiny pate in bewilderment. "Never seen anything like it."

"Tell me about it," Sam muttered, carefully hiding his amusement.

"When's the kid due, Sam?" Jack asked. Unlike the others, Jack seemed to get more cheerful and optimistic with each beer.

Sam shrugged and scowled. "Another month or so, I think. She said, but I forgot."

"You forgot?" Jack echoed, looking startled.

"Yeah. At least, I keep trying to forget," Sam added with a twisted smile.

"Not real happy about it, huh?" Talley inquired.

Sam shook his head. "It wasn't my idea."

"Wouldn't have been mine, either," Talley fervently agreed. "Ain't no woman tying me down to a houseful of whining brats to support. My brother's working three jobs now to keep his daughter in beauty-pageant dresses. Beauty pageants," he repeated in disgust. "The kid's ten years old, looks like she's been splattered with freckle paint and is twenty pounds overweight, thanks to her pampering mama. Put her in one of those ruffled satin pageant dresses and she looks like an over-stuffed sofa pillow with Shirley Temple curls."

"She ever win any of the pageants?" Jack asked.

"Hell, no. My sister-in-law keeps saying it's all politics. Claims little Melisande can't win because they ain't rich. She just can't accept that the kid's ugly."

Sam choked on a swig of beer. He'd have to relate that story to Dallas, he thought with a hidden smile. She'd get a kick out of it.

Then he brought himself sharply back into character. "I ain't working three jobs," he grumbled. "This one's bad enough."

Jack nodded, his cheerful mood affected by the others' pessimism. "I just hope I can make my wife wait to have kids until I finish computer-repair school. I really want to work at an inside job. I want air-conditioning," he added wistfully, wiping his brow as though still affected by the vicious heat of his workday.

R.J. looked thoughtful. "Oh, it ain't so bad," he offered. "I didn't like it when my wife was pregnant, but we got us a couple of good kids. Two boys," he added for Sam's benefit. "Nine and seven. The oldest one's already one hell of a baseball player. Little one likes soccer. They play on city leagues."

Jack perked up visibly. "Yeah, Sam," he said. "You'll like that, won't you? Throwing a ball around with your kid?"

Sam sighed heavily. "Doctor says it's probably a girl," he complained. "Just what I need. Another griping woman in the house."

The other three men nodded in sympathy. Sam tried very hard not to picture Dallas's reaction to the painfully chauvinistic turn the conversation had just taken.

This next part was going to be tricky. He needed to try to elicit information without arousing suspicions—or alienating his sources. He sighed heavily and stared into his beer, trying to project the image of utter dejection. "I just wish this hadn't happened," he said. "I can't afford this right now. I really didn't want it."

There was an awkward pause as his three co-workers digested his misery.

Jack was the first to speak. "Have you considered giving it up for adoption?"

Sam shrugged. "Dallas didn't want to talk about it. Anyway, I hear all the red tape and everything gets pretty complicated. I don't want to mess with no damned bureaucrats."

"There's private adoption," R.J. suggested. "That's easier, I hear. All you need is an attorney."

"I hate lawyers worse than I hate bureaucrats," Sam pronounced scornfully.

"If it was me, I'd just take off," Talley boasted. "Hell, your woman's the one who got herself knocked up. Probably did it on purpose. Let her deal with it. If you're gone, she can get on government assistance, probably rake in more than you're getting busting your butt on a construction crew. Get yourself free, man."

R.J. frowned, and Jack looked taken aback by Talley's callous suggestion. Sam only nodded. "Don't think it hasn't crossed my mind," he said.

"Have another beer," Talley urged, seeming pleased by Sam's concurrence with his attitude. "Nothing for you to hurry home to, is there?"

"Not a thing," Sam agreed. He waved an arm to motion for the bored, sour-faced waitress who'd been unenthusiastically serving them during the past couple of hours. "Hey, Wilma. Bring us another round!"

He'd struck out, he decided, as Wilma frowned even more heavily and nodded in answer to his bellow. These guys either knew nothing about the baby-selling ring allegedly working in their neighborhood or they weren't the type to send anyone to them. R.J. and Jack were both hardworking stiffs who tried to live right—at least most of the time. Talley was a jerk, but still rather naive in some ways; viewed his surroundings through blinders he'd deliberately donned to block out anything he didn't want to see.

Apparently Talley was right about one thing, though: Sam was busting his butt on a construction crew for no good reason.

Looked like it was about time to begin part two of the investigation—which started with getting himself fired. But that would have to wait until Monday. Tonight he could sit back, relax, and allow Sam Pulaski to have another couple of beers with his co-workers. And then he'd better be heading back to the apartment to check in with Dallas.

He was sure she'd understand that he'd spent the evening working on the investigation, even if the results had come up negative this time.

AFTER ONE OF THE LONGEST, most boring and uncomfortable evenings she'd ever spent, Dallas finally heard a noise outside her apartment. Since she was wearing the pregnancy harness—she hadn't wanted to risk going without it until Sam returned—she snatched open the door before he had a chance to insert his key. "Well, it's about time! Where the... Oh. Polly, it's you. I thought you were Sam."

Polly looked up from the floor of the hallway, where she was crouched over a clutter of what looked like items from the oversize purse she always carried. "Spilled my damned purse looking for my keys," she explained, then cocked her dark head and asked, "Sam ain't home yet?"

"No," Dallas said. "And I'm getting worried," she added, the words only halfway for Polly's benefit. Actually, Dallas *was* getting a bit concerned about Sam. Had he pursued a lead that had landed him in trouble? Had he stumbled onto something dangerous while playing the Lone Ranger without her?

"Probably out at a bar somewhere," Polly said. "That's where most of the guys around here end up on Friday night. Get their paychecks and can't wait to spend them."

"Oh, Sam wouldn't do that," Dallas said, wringing her hands affectingly in front of her. "He knows how badly we need his paycheck just for food and baby supplies."

"Yeah, right, kid." Polly stretched awkwardly for the items scattered around her, trying to stuff them back into the black-and-purple vinyl handbag.

"Here, let me help you." Dallas bent quickly to help, then gasped and put out a hand to steady herself on the grimy floor when she nearly fell right on her face from the weight of the harness.

Polly's hand shot out to catch Dallas's shoulder. "You okay?"

"Yes, I'm fine." Still kneeling, Dallas shook her head. "Can't believe I did that."

"You shouldn't be bending so fast," Polly scolded. "You know your balance is off."

"I keep forgetting," Dallas explained, reaching for a tube of lipstick.

Polly looked surprised. "How the hell could you forget? It ain't like you haven't been in this shape for a while."

Mentally chiding herself for the slip, Dallas made a face. "It must be Freudian," she said lightly.

Polly smiled. "Yeah, I know what you mean. There's times I wish I could just pretend I wasn't in this shape and I'd suddenly have my own body back."

Dallas handed Polly the items she'd gathered, then struggled awkwardly to her feet. She patted her solid "tummy." "I guess I shouldn't complain so much," she said. "Sam says I'm always griping about something."

"Sam's a—" Polly bit back whatever she'd started to say, though it obviously wasn't easy for her. She took a deep breath and rose to her own feet with Dallas's assistance. "Look, if you need anything tonight, come on down to my place, okay?" she said, instead. "I mean, in case Sam stays out all night and you get scared. Or in case he comes home drunk and mean. Whatever, you can come to me, okay?"

The hooker with a heart of gold, Dallas thought flippantly, then regretted the thought when she saw the sincerity in Polly's overly-emphasized eyes. How long had it been since Polly had offered a hand of friendship to anyone? And how long since that offer had been accepted with a smile rather than a slap of rejection?

Dallas smiled. "Thank you, Polly," she said gently. "But I'm sure I'll be fine. Sam yells a lot, but he would never hurt me. He probably just had to work late."

Polly looked torn between pity and impatience with Dallas's naiveté. "Okay. Just remember what I said."

"I will. Thank you."

Polly nodded and moved on, one hand pressed to the small of her back, her swollen feet wobbling in the too-high heels. Dallas watched for a moment, then went back inside, shaking her head at Polly's stubborn insistence on wearing shoes that had to be causing her agony in her condition. She felt rather guilty for sulking all evening over wearing the harness. At least she could take it off and rest once Sam returned. At least she didn't have swollen breasts and ankles and cramps and hemorrhoids and all that other terrible stuff Polly had described.

She spent the next half hour pacing, and remembering how Sam had looked with a gun pressed to his ear the last time she'd worked with him and things had gone horribly wrong. It had been a drug bust, the result of a week's work on their parts. Dallas had never quite understood how everything had gone so wrong at the last moment, but Sam had narrowly avoided being shot— and she'd come much too close for comfort, herself. She'd saved his butt that time—and, okay, he'd saved hers, too—but he was on his own now. What had he gotten himself into?

And why on earth was she so terribly worried about it? He was just her partner, and a temporary one at that. She was acting as though he really *was* her lover and the father of her "child"!

Finally his key sounded in the lock. Nerves stretched to the limit, Dallas whirled to face him. He entered with a slightly unsteady walk, rather glazed eyes, a dopey grin and the heavy aroma of cheap beer. "Hi, honey," he said, the words a bit slurred. "I'm home."

Dallas's temper exploded.

6

"WHERE THE HELL HAVE you been? Do you have any idea what time it is?"

Sam blinked in surprise at the anger in Dallas's voice. He closed the door behind him. "I—uh—had a couple of drinks with some of the guys from work."

Fists doubled on her hips, she glared at him. "You were having drinks? That's it? *Drinks?*"

"I had a sandwich, too," he offered, as though that would make it better.

"A sandwich?" Dallas knew her voice was rising, but was having trouble controlling it. "I made fettuccine Alfredo. Do you know what fettuccine Alfredo tastes like after it's been sitting on the table for four hours? Wallpaper paste, that's what!"

"Look, I'm sorry, but I—"

"You couldn't call to let me know you were going to be late?"

"Dallas, we don't have a phone."

"Don't give me excuses!" she yelled, stamping one foot. "I've been going nuts sitting here in this ugly apartment with nothing to do but try to remember what my feet look like, and no one to talk to but a couple of cockroaches. I waited to eat with you, but then the food got cold and disgusting and now I'm starving. For all I knew, you could have been lying dead somewhere. Did you care that I might be worried? Did you even *try* to let me know where you were? No!"

"But I—"

"You think it's fun sitting around this place? You think it's easy carrying twenty pounds of extra weight in front of me? You think it's a breeze to try to cook around this thing? Then *you* try it! See how *you* like it."

"Dallas, I—"

"You probably weren't even working," she added, on a roll now. "You probably didn't ask even one question about—mmph."

Sam's hand was planted firmly over her mouth. He loomed over her, gazing narrowly down at her, his goofy grin replaced by a frown.

"I was working," he said, his voice much quieter than hers had been. "And I did ask questions. Enough, at least, to know that there aren't any easy answers to be found on the construction crew. Now, would you watch what you're saying, for crying out loud? I know you're trying to make this sound good, but don't get carried away and forget to be discreet, okay?"

Dallas hadn't thought she could get any madder. She was wrong. She shoved his hand away from her face. "Don't you *ever* cover my mouth with your hand again! And stop telling me how to do my—mmph!"

Sam didn't silence her with his hand this time. He used his mouth.

The heat of anger transformed itself rapidly, almost magically into passion. Without even stopping to think about it, Dallas threw herself into the kiss with the same enthusiasm she'd put into her tantrum.

Sam seemed a bit surprised at first by her cooperation, but then he took full advantage of the opportunity, parting her lips with his tongue to deepen the kiss,
his arms closing around her. Both of them murmured
their frustration at the bulky padding that separated
them when they would have pressed closer together.

Sam's hands slid down Dallas's back, settling on her
hips to hold her as closely against him as possible. She
looped her arms around his neck, strained over the
padding between them and lost herself in his kiss. She
had to admit that she'd been wanting to kiss him again
ever since he'd kissed her that morning, even if he'd
only been performing then for any onlookers' benefit.

There were no onlookers now.

Sam's thick, sandy hair was soft against her fingers
when she buried them at the back of his head. His
mouth was hard, hot, skillful. As far as kisses went, this
one would have earned him an A-plus, she thought
dreamily, sliding her tongue tantalizingly against his.
He tasted of beer, and she never would have dreamed
the combination would be so pleasing. Or was it just
the taste of Sam that intrigued her so?

Her mind was spinning by the time he finally, reluctantly ended the kiss. He lifted his head slowly, his eyes
locked with hers. She searched his face, wondering
what he was thinking, what he was feeling as he stared
back down at her. She thought she saw there the same
stunned realization that was overwhelming her.

The exchange between them, explosive as it had
been, hadn't been a total surprise to Dallas. The attraction had been building for a long time—weeks,
months, maybe—though she'd fought hard against it.

She had refused to acknowledge it even to herself—until now, when she could no longer deny it.

Sam seemed to suddenly become aware that he was still holding her, his hands still clasped on her hips. He dropped his arms abruptly. "I, uh, I'd better take a shower," he murmured, his voice rather hoarse.

Dallas could only nod, not trusting her voice at all.

He hesitated another moment, still looking at her, and then he took a sharp breath, turned, and all but bolted for the shower.

Dallas covered her flaming cheeks with her hands and moaned.

And she'd thought their *last* assignment together had gotten complicated!

DALLAS THREW OUT THE fettuccine, still too stunned to feel more than a flicker of renewed irritation that she was having to do so. She made herself a turkey sandwich, then realized that her hunger had faded along with her temper. She choked down half of it, stuffed the remainder into a plastic sandwich bag, and shoved it in the refrigerator for later.

She was tired. Mentally and physically exhausted. Sitting alone for long, boring hours was almost more wearing for her than steady physical activity.

Her nightshirt in her hand, she was waiting at the door of the bathroom when Sam emerged after his shower, wearing only the gym shorts he favored for sleeping. She brushed past him with an incoherent murmur, her gaze trained firmly away from his bare chest and legs. She spent a long time brushing her teeth, removing her makeup and donning her nightshirt. As always, she gave a sigh of relief when she removed the heavy harness. Taking that thing off was better—and faster—than a strict diet for making her feel slim and fit.

Sam was sitting on his side of the bed when she finally left the bathroom. He looked tired, she noted. There were deep lines around his hazel eyes and unsmiling mouth, and a weary slump in his bare shoulders. His very sexy bare shoulders, she thought before she could stop herself. She turned her eyes away and moved around to her side of the bed.

They crawled under the sheets without speaking. Sam reached out to snap off the bedside lamp, and the room was thrown into darkness. Someone walked noisily above them, a baby cried somewhere beneath them. Someone was playing a stereo too loudly, heavy on the bass. The sounds of traffic, shouts, and an occasional siren drifted in from outside.

There was total silence inside the bedroom.

Dallas could almost hear the minutes ticking by. Slowly. Painfully slowly. She lay on her back, staring wide-eyed at the ceiling. Sleep seemed very far away. She was just about to give up and go watch television when Sam spoke, his voice sounding startlingly loud.

"Dallas?"

She moistened her lips. "Yeah?"

"Sorry about dinner. The guys asked me to have a few beers with them and it seemed like a good chance to pump them for information."

She covered her face with her hands and groaned deeply.

Sam sounded startled when he spoke again. "Dallas? What's wrong? Are you still mad?"

"I'm mad at myself," she muttered, her voice muffled by her hands. "I can't believe I yelled at you like that. Of course, you were just doing your job—you did exactly what Sam Pulaski would have done. I don't know why I got so furious. I guess I got carried away with my role."

Sam exhaled deeply—what might have been a sigh of relief that she wasn't still angry with him. "It's okay," he said. "I understand. Sometimes it's easy to forget who you are for a while. Besides, you were probably bored out of your mind. I know I would have been if I'd had to sit alone in this dump all day and all evening."

"Yeah, I was," she admitted. "This assignment doesn't seem to be going anywhere. Sometimes I wonder if we're just wasting our time."

"It's only been five days," Sam reminded her. "Brashear expected us to take a couple of weeks to firmly establish our cover. And you have made a lot of headway with Polly. She's already talking to you. If she's involved in this, you'll know soon."

He was trying to be encouraging, but Dallas didn't feel much better. "I still feel stupid," she said. "Not for yelling at you—I needed to do that for the cover. But I was really mad at you for missing dinner."

Sam chuckled and rolled up to one elbow, propping his head on his hand as he looked down at her. "You really did get carried away with your role, didn't you?"

She nodded against the pillow. "I spent the day cleaning the refrigerator," she confessed. "I even pulled it out and mopped behind it. At one point, I stopped and asked myself if I ought to be doing heavy cleaning in my condition!"

Sam laughed softly.

But Dallas wasn't through. "You know what I found myself doing this afternoon to entertain myself? Choosing names for the baby! I tell you, Perry, we've got to get on with this case before I start decorating the place with cutesy country craft stuff."

Sam was still laughing. "Naming the kid, huh? So what did you choose?"

She sighed and mentally cursed herself for being so candid with him. Now she'd probably never hear the end of it. "Never mind."

"How about Bob? I've always liked Bob."

"Bob?" she repeated. "For a baby?"

"Sure. It's simple, easy to spell, a nice strong, manly name. Like Sam," he added.

"I can see why simple, easy to spell, and monosyllabic would appeal to you."

He growled in response to the less-than-subtle insult. "Watch it, Sanders." And then he reached out almost absently and brushed a strand of hair from her cheek as he continued the teasing. "I suppose you'd rather name your kid after a city? Atlanta, maybe? Detroit?"

"Are you making fun of my name, Perry?"

"Would I do that?"

"You would."

"So where'd you get the name Dallas, anyway?"

"That's where my mother dumped me," she answered with a shrug against the pillows. "I guess it seemed appropriate to some social worker with a twisted sense of humor."

Sam stopped laughing. "You were never adopted?"

"No. I grew up in foster homes. Most of them were okay. Some sucked. But that's life, I guess."

"I'm sorry."

She shook her head fervently, dislodging his hand, which had rested against her cheek. "No pity, Perry. I really hate pity."

"Stop being so prickly, Sanders. It isn't pity. It's just commiseration. That's allowed between friends, isn't it?"

"Friends?" she repeated thoughtfully, trying to focus on his face through the dim, watery light coming in through the window curtains. "Since when are we friends?"

"I don't know," he murmured, moving his fingers back to her cheek. "But it seems to have happened somehow. You have any objections?"

"Not to being friends," she answered cautiously.

His head was very close to hers now—so close she could feel his warm breath caressing her right cheek as softly as his fingers stroked her left. "What if we became more than friends?" he asked, very quietly. "Would you have any objections to that?"

"I—" She had to stop to clear her throat. "I think that would be a mistake."

He toyed with her left earlobe, tracing it with one fingertip. "Do you?"

"Yes," she whispered, then said it again, more firmly. "Yes. Definitely."

"Why?"

"I'm lousy with relationships. Every time I've tried it, something went wrong. *Really* wrong," she emphasized, to make sure he got her point. "You and I have several strikes against us already. Let's not get completely carried away with this assignment and take a chance on turning it into a bigger disaster than the last one."

"What are the strikes against us?" he asked, sounding genuinely curious.

She couldn't believe he didn't already know. Maybe he just wanted confirmation of what he already suspected. "We're cops, for one thing. Cops have a history of bad relationships. You should already know that," she added, remembering that he'd been living with someone when she'd met him. One of their coworkers had mentioned it right after Dallas and Sam had been introduced on her first day in his precinct. She'd immediately stifled any initial attraction she might have felt for the sandy-haired, hazel-eyed detective; she had very strict rules about "trespassing."

By the time she'd learned that Sam and his former roommate had gone separate ways, she had pushed that early attraction firmly aside. Permanently, she'd thought. Obviously, she'd been mistaken.

"Granted, cops have some problems with relationships," Sam conceded. "Usually because the other person doesn't understand what it's like being a cop. What else?"

"We don't get along. You're always grouchy, and I like to laugh. You always try to tell me what to do—I don't like taking orders from anyone, especially my partner."

"I'm aware that I tend to be bossy. I've been working on that with you, or haven't you noticed? As for my personality, I don't think I'm any grouchier than you are. You just see it more with me than with yourself."

"Bull."

"And who was it attacking whom earlier this evening?" he asked politely.

She flushed. "That doesn't count. I've already said I wasn't myself then."

"Guess I just bring out the worst in you."

"Exactly," she said, feeling as though another point had just been made to support her argument.

"Okay, so I'm a grouchy, bossy cop. Anything else about me you don't like? You think I'm ugly? Stupid, maybe?"

She frowned. "Of course, I don't think you're ugly. And you aren't stupid. You're one hell of a good cop—when you aren't busy trying to do my job for me. But—"

"I don't think you're ugly, either," Sam interrupted, nuzzling her cheek with his nose. "In fact," he added, his lips brushing the corner of her mouth, "I think you're gorgeous. I always have. It just took me a while to realize that I like the rest of you almost as much as that great bod of yours."

Sam was calling her gorgeous? If she weren't so damned flattered, she would probably be suspicious of his motives. He'd never given her flowery compliments before, never touched her the way he was touching her now, sending little surges of electricity rippling through her. It was almost enough to make her wonder what he was really after.

And then she remembered what else he'd claimed. "You don't like me, Perry," she stated automatically. "You think I'm a pain in the butt."

"Well, yes," he agreed. "But I like you, anyway. Funny, huh?"

"I don't—"

Her words were smothered by his kiss.

It was a long time before he lifted his head—at least, as far as he *could* lift it with Dallas clinging like a tightly knotted tie around his neck. "Oh, yeah, Sanders," he murmured, gathering her closer. "I like you."

He kissed her again. And then again. And before long, it was hard to tell who was kissing whom, whose arms were more hungry, whose movements more urgent.

Dallas's nightshirt tangled around her waist, baring her thighs to Sam's seeking hands. His chest was warm and sleek beneath her palms, his legs rough and hard as they tangled with hers. And then her nightshirt and her panties were on the floor, and Sam's mouth moved against her breasts, his fingers wandering into the thatch of brown hair between her legs. Dallas arched into him, gasping her pleasure—and her bemusement.

Again and again he kissed her—her breasts, her mouth, her neck, her stomach. And then he moved lower.

Her fingers knotted in his shaggy hair, Dallas tried to tell herself that she could bring an end to this at any time. Sam hadn't even removed his shorts yet. All she had to do was tell him to stop.

But she didn't want him to stop.

Maybe the assignment really had warped her brain. Maybe she'd spent too many nights sleeping in the same bed with Sam. Or maybe she was finally giving in to an attraction she'd been fighting for a very long time. But she didn't want him to stop.

She tugged at his hair, pulling him into her arms. And then she kissed him in a way that let him know exactly what she wanted. Sam murmured his approval into her mouth.

She reached for the waistband of his gym shorts and pushed them downward.

"Dallas," Sam groaned, his body already straining to join with hers. "I wasn't prepared for this. I can't protect you."

"I take care of my own protection, Perry," Dallas whispered, wrapping her legs around his hips. "And I want this. I want *you*."

"I want you, too. More than I think I've ever wanted before," he admitted, sliding his fingers into her tumbled hair.

"Then what are you waiting for?" she asked him softly.

He smiled against her mouth. And then he waited no longer.

HER BODY HEAVY WITH repletion, Dallas stirred against Sam's shoulder. He lay sprawled beneath her, his breathing not quite steady, his heart still racing beneath her cheek. Intimately tangled with hers, his body glistened with a fine sheen of perspiration, and his hair was damp around his neck when she touched it with her fingertips.

It was nice to know that he'd found as much satisfaction as she had with their lovemaking, she thought contentedly.

Her eyelids were growing heavy. The sounds outside the bedroom began to fade as she drifted toward unconsciousness. But there was one more thing she wanted to say before she fell asleep. "Perry?"

"Hmm?" His own voice was slurred, sleepy.

"I like you, too."

He hugged her roughly against him, and this time there was a smile in his voice when he said, "Go to sleep, Sanders."

She smiled against his throat and decided that just this once, she'd do as he suggested without argument.

SAM WAS WATCHING DALLAS sleep again. He lay on his side, facing her, his gaze focused unblinkingly on her sweetly relaxed face. He knew she wouldn't like it that he was staring at her at such a vulnerable, unguarded moment, but he couldn't seem to look away.

He had absolutely no idea how to handle this new development between them. Making love with her had been— Well, it had been incredible. Spectacular. Staggering. As a matter of fact, he would like very much to do it again. Soon. Repeatedly. But was that all there was between them? Sexual chemistry? And if so, how come it hadn't hit him before? Why had he only fully realized it after he'd become aware of all the other things he admired about her?

Maybe there was more to it than sex. And wasn't *that* a scary thought?

She stirred against the pillow, her fine brown hair tangling softly around her face. He wanted to reach out and smooth it back, but was afraid he'd wake her if he did. She needed her rest.

He didn't blame her for being bored and restless during the past week. As skilled as she was in the kitchen, Dallas wasn't the type to content herself for long with repetitive domestic routines. She thrived on action, pressure, even a hint of danger. Dallas loved her job in a way that Sam could only envy. If he'd ever really felt that way about his career, the enthusiasm had burned out years ago. He hadn't felt particularly enthusiastic about anything for a long time—until last night. Making love with Dallas Sanders had made him feel more intensely alive, more passionately aware, than he'd felt in years.

Now he found himself already dreading the inevitable return to the dull, gray, smothering monotony of life without her. Because something told him that the end of this assignment would also mark the end of whatever tentative relationship had been formed between him and his impulsive, utterly dedicated partner.

She stirred again, yawned, then blinked sleepily a couple of times. Her gaze met his and suddenly focused. Sam could almost watch the awareness returning to her in stages as she realized that he was lying beside her, watching her, and that she wasn't wearing anything. And then her eyes opened wide, and he knew she'd remembered exactly what had happened between them last night.

How would she react? Would she withdraw in panic? Turn her confusion into anger at him? Brush it off as "just one of those things"?

He hadn't expected her to smile.

"Good morning," she murmured.

"Good morning." He noticed how soft and inviting her unpainted mouth looked first thing in the morning.

"Did you sleep well?" she asked politely.

"Yes. You?"

"Mmm. Very." She stretched lazily and the sheet slid down to expose the upper curves of her small, perfect breasts. Sam felt his heart do a slow somersault in his chest.

And then she smiled again. "I haven't slept that well in a very long time," she assured him.

He couldn't resist reaching out to touch her. He restricted himself to brushing back that lock of hair that had been tempting him all morning. "Neither have I."

"Are you hungry? I was thinking of making waffles for breakfast."

Waffles were very far down on his list of priorities just then. He looked again at her smile, threw caution to the wind and reached for her.

"Maybe we could talk about breakfast later," he whispered, his mouth hovering a breath above hers.

Dallas wound her arms around his neck. "Sounds good to me," she agreed with flattering eagerness.

7

THAT WEEKEND, FOR THE first time, he found himself almost wanting to believe the fantasy he was living.

He and Dallas spent most of Saturday in the bedroom. They made love—repeatedly. They talked, they raided the kitchen for snacks, which they fed each other in bed. They laughed. He noticed at one point that Dallas was looking at him strangely, though she'd been giggling only moments before. "What is it?" he asked, trailing a lazy hand down her firm, bare thigh.

"You're laughing," she said, sounding bemused.

"Yeah, well, you're pretty funny, Sanders."

"You don't laugh very often. Except for the first time you saw me in the pregnancy harness, I don't think I'd ever really heard you laugh before."

His smile changed to a quick frown. "Sure you have."

She shook her head. "I've heard you chuckle. I've seen you smile—very rarely. But I'm not sure you've ever really laughed out loud around me before last week."

She was making him self-conscious. He shrugged.

"You're a very serious guy, aren't you, Perry? Aren't you happy?" she asked lightly. He sensed that she was only half teasing.

His head propped on one hand, he touched her face with the fingertips of his other hand. "I'm happy right now," he said quietly. And realized, to his surprise, that he meant it.

She smiled and nestled her cheek into his palm. "That's nice," she murmured, her lips moving against his caressing thumb.

"Mmm. Nice," he agreed, his voice growing husky. His body stirring. Again. "Very nice," he whispered, and replaced his thumb with his mouth.

She wrapped her arms around him and pulled him down to her.

THEY TALKED ABOUT MOVIES. Sports. Mutual friends. And then Dallas wanted to know what kind of music Sam listened to.

"Classic rock, usually. Why?"

"Just curious," she murmured around a bite of home-made brownie, part of the batch she'd made while struggling to entertain herself Friday afternoon. "I'd have a hard time sleeping with someone who regularly listened to Roger Whittaker," she added after swallowing.

Sam smiled and brushed chocolate crumbs off his bare stomach. "A music snob, Sanders?"

"Yep," she admitted unabashedly. "And, by the way, if you don't like Foreigner, then I'm afraid it's over between us. I have to set standards, you know."

"Then I guess it's a good thing I like Foreigner, isn't it?"

She made a great show of sighing in relief and wiping her brow. "Made it past the first hurdle. So, how do you feel about science fiction?"

He really liked science fiction, he assured her—but he had to confess to a slight preference for tightly written mystery novels. She graciously allowed him that eccentricity.

"What else do you like to do, Dallas? Besides read sci-fi."

She shrugged. "I work," she said simply.

"That's it?"

"Pretty much. Who has time for anything else?"

She didn't sound as though she were really complaining. Sam knew it was because Dallas truly loved her work. Again, he felt that uncomfortable ripple of envy that he didn't—couldn't—feel the same way about their mutual career. It was a job to him. A way to pay the bills. That was all it had ever been. He sensed that, for Dallas, it had always been much more.

They worked together to prepare dinner Saturday evening. Dallas broiled two inexpensive steaks, promising that her special marinade would make them taste like the finest cuts of beef. Sam made a salad and prepared a dressing from a recipe he solemnly swore had been passed down for eleven generations in his family, to be revealed to outsiders only at the risk of great personal injury.

"Eleven generations, hmm?" Dallas asked skeptically, trying to see around him to watch what he was adding to the bowl.

"Eleven," he repeated, blocking her view with his broad shoulders.

"And only your relatives know the recipe?"

"It has never been divulged to anyone outside the Perry family."

"What about people who marry into the Perry family?"

"They are given the secret on their wedding nights."

"And if they decide to divorce the Perry they married in order to receive the secret?"

"Then they have to be killed," Sam assured her gravely. "There are very few divorces in my family."

"You'll tell Junior, won't you?" she asked, patting her flat stomach beneath the oversize white T-shirt that was all she wore at that moment. The shirt belonged to Sam. He liked the way it looked on her much better than on him, he thought rather dreamily.

"Sam?"

"Mmm?"

"You will tell Junior the secret recipe, won't you?" she prodded, smiling at their silliness. "After all, he *is* your child."

"I'll tell him," Sam promised. "The usual method— a secret ceremony for all the adult males in the family, to be held at midnight on his twenty-first birthday."

"Only adult males? Why, you sexist pig. What if Junior's a girl, hmm?"

Sam shook his head. "Bob isn't a girl," he announced flatly.

"We are *not* naming this child Bob," Dallas informed him.

He sighed noisily. "I don't understand this antipathy you have toward the name Bob. It's really a great name, Sanders."

"I know. Short, simple, easy to spell."

"Yeah. Frontward and backward. What more could you ask?"

"Creativity? Imagination?"

He shook his head again. "People with creative and imaginative names usually end up getting teased. No one makes fun of good, solid names like Bob."

"Or Sam, I suppose."

"Right."

She snorted. "You've got no imagination at all, Perry."

"Oh, I don't know," he murmured, glancing at her over his shoulder. "I'm imagining a couple of interesting things I'd like to do with you."

She widened her eyes. "Something we haven't already tried?"

"Honey, we haven't even gotten good and started."

"Oh, my." She fanned herself rapidly with one hand. "I'm getting all flustered. Um—just how hungry are you, anyway?"

He laughed and turned back to his salad. "You can just wait until after dinner, Sanders. A man needs his strength for the activities I have in mind."

"Why don't I whip you up a liver milk shake to go with that? Some oysters, maybe?"

Sam realized that he was laughing again.

Damn, it felt good.

THEY PLAYED CARDS AFTER dinner. It turned out that they shared a mutual passion for gin rummy—and a mutual competitiveness that turned the simple game into a grimly serious contest. Neither of them liked to lose. They diplomatically decided to end play at a point when the scores were tied.

Sam watched the evening news before turning in, admitting that he wanted to check the scores of that day's professional baseball games. He had a bet riding on one of them, he confessed.

"A bet?" Dallas repeated, her head coming up from its comfortable position on his thigh. She'd stretched out beside him on the couch, her feet dangling over the opposite end, and she was totally uninterested in sports news.

"Chill out, Sanders. I'm not talking about bookies, here. The bet's with Walter. And the loser has to buy the winner a steak dinner. So don't start reading me my rights, okay?"

"I wasn't accusing you of illegal gambling," she retorted, resting her head on his leg again. "You're too much a straight arrow for anything like that. And much too unimaginative," she added.

"Unimaginative?" he echoed, feigning offense. "Who, me?"

"Hey, you're the one who wants to name the kid Bob. If the adjective fits, wear it."

"Okay, 'fess up, Sanders. You once knew someone named Bob, didn't you? What did he do, break your heart?"

"I have nothing personal against the name Bob," she argued. "It's just—well, dull."

"Dull?" He tapped one finger firmly against the wooden arm of the couch. "Like Sam, perhaps?"

"The name or the person?" she inquired sweetly.

"You're treading on dangerous ground here, Sanders. Sam is a fine old name in my family. It's been passed down—"

"For eleven generations, I know," Dallas cut in with a roll of her eyes.

"Three," he corrected her. "Starting with my grandfather."

"Then I'm surprised you don't want to name your kid Sam the Fourth."

"I do have more imagination than that."

She giggled. "Oh, yeah. Right. Bob."

"Okay, so what would *you* name the kid? Something weird, right? Like Artemis. Or Zeus. Or Vladislav."

"All fine old names," she declared virtuously. "But my favorite male name is Peter. After my favorite actor of all time, Peter O'Toole."

Sam choked. "Peter Perry? Give me a break, Dallas, the kid would be the laughingstock of his kindergarten class."

To his surprise, she actually blushed, her cheeks turning an intriguingly rosy color. "I hadn't thought of using your last name," she muttered. "This is a hypothetical kid, remember?"

"Right. A hypothetical kid who would be called Peter Pulaski. I hate to break this to you, but that isn't any better."

"This is ridiculous," Dallas said, sitting up abruptly. "There *is* no kid! And, besides, it might be a girl," she added, obviously without stopping to think.

Sam laughed. "I suppose if it's a girl, you'd want to name it Penny?"

"I'm going to brush my teeth," she announced, sweeping toward the bedroom door with exaggerated dignity. "Watch your scores, Perry. You're probably going to be buying Walter a steak dinner before long."

He was still grinning when she left the room.

Sanders was cute when she was embarrassed. She would seriously hurt him, of course, if he dared say so aloud.

He found himself suddenly picturing a tiny little girl with Dallas's brilliant blue eyes and intriguing dimples. His grin vanished.

Now where on earth had that image come from? And why the hell had it left him with this achy, hollow feeling somewhere deep inside his chest?

SAM HAD PUT HIS momentary melancholy firmly behind him by the time he and Dallas crawled back into bed. He turned to take her into his arms, and she came to him eagerly.

Above them, a bed began to creak.

"*Oh, yes. Yes, yes, oh, God, yes!*" came the familiar shriek.

Dallas dissolved into giggles against Sam's chest.

His deep laughter echoed from the dark corners of the grubby little room.

SAM SLIPPED DOWNSTAIRS for a newspaper early Sunday morning. The little old woman he'd spotted once before was moving down the first floor hallway behind her walker, wearing the same faded housedress and probably the same baggy knee-high stockings. He gave her a bright smile. "Good morning."

She darted him a suspicious look and redoubled her pace, the walker thump-thumping loudly on the linoleum floor.

Sam chuckled and tucked the newspaper under his arm. Sam Pulaski certainly wasn't making any new friends in this building. But Sam Perry had surprisingly few complaints at the moment. He felt better than he'd felt in longer than he could remember. He'd just spent one of the most spectacular nights in his experience. Dallas was upstairs even now making waffles for their breakfast. They had the entire day ahead of them—just the two of them.

He could almost believe it was all true. That he and Dallas were a couple, making a home together, no matter how modest their surroundings. That the rapport they'd established extended beyond the bedroom, beyond the physical hunger they hadn't begun to sate. That it wouldn't all come to a messy, awkward, embarrassing end.

Hell, he could almost believe in little "Bob."

He shook his head, some of his good mood fading. This was getting dangerous. And he wasn't talking about their assignment.

Dallas looked up with a smile when he joined her in the kitchen. The heavenly scent of crisply browned waffles filled the air, making his mouth water. But it was the warm smile she gave him that whetted his most urgent hunger.

Oh, yes, he thought grimly. This was most definitely getting dangerous.

It was the first time any assignment had ever put his heart at risk.

"DEAR ELLIE," the letter in the newspaper began. "I'm in love with a man who can't seem to open up to me. I want to make a lifelong commitment to him, but every time I try to talk about his feelings for me or our relationship, he changes the subject. Is there any hope for us? Signed, Frustrated."

Dallas peeked over the top of the newspaper page at Sam, who sat at the other end of the couch, perusing the sports section. As though he'd sensed her looking at him, he glanced up. He smiled—that crooked, lazy smile that made her stomach do slow somersaults. She returned the smile with a weak attempt of her own, and slid her gaze quickly back to the features-section page she'd been reading. Sam looked down at his baseball scores again.

"Dear Frustrated," Dallas read silently. "A man who won't open up often has something to hide. A lasting relationship is built on total communication. Talk to him. If he still won't discuss your future, you may have to accept that he doesn't share your feelings or your goals. I urge you to find out now, before you invest any more in this one-sided relationship."

Total communication. Dallas sneaked another look over the paper, studying Sam's attractive profile. She couldn't say she and Sam shared total communication. Not verbally, anyway. They communicated beautifully in bed—but shouldn't there be more to it than that?

There was so much about him she didn't know. He'd told her about his childhood, growing up the beloved only son of a police-officer father and a homemaker mother. He'd told her that he'd joined the police force nine years ago, and had vaguely mentioned that he'd first graduated from a state university. He'd brushed off her questions about his college major. He didn't seem to enjoy talking about his career achievements.

There was a darkness in him, a deep, secret pain that she sometimes saw in his hazel eyes or sensed in his deep, gruff voice. She'd once thought it had something to do with his broken relationship with the woman he'd lived with when she'd first met him. Now she wasn't so sure. When he mentioned Paula, which he'd done only a couple of times since she'd known him, there'd been no real heartache or deep longing in his voice. As far as she could tell, he'd been fond of the woman, but he hadn't been devastated when the affair had ended. Dallas suspected that the breakup had been as much his decision as Paula's.

Had there been another woman, before Paula? Had someone else hurt him so badly that he was still stinging, still wary about getting involved with anyone else?

She didn't like to think about Sam mourning an old love even when he was holding her in his arms.

Not that she was ready for a lifelong commitment, either, Dallas assured herself hastily, closing the newspaper section. Her record with relationships was abysmal, and most of the men she'd known had been heartaches waiting to happen. Or vicious animals just waiting for an opportunity to attack. Or heartless sleazoids who viewed women as nothing more than vulnerable bodies to be used for their own sick, selfish pleasures.

She suppressed a shudder as several old, ugly memories surfaced from the deep recesses of her mind. She pushed them firmly back into their dark corners, where she preferred them to remain.

Sam Perry had his secrets. Dallas Sanders had hers. This so-called relationship was nothing more than a pleasant diversion to occupy them during an otherwise slow-moving investigation. When the assignment was over, their affair would end, as well. She could only hope it would end amicably, without an ugly scene that would make it more difficult for them to continue to work together.

"Aren't you supposed to get in touch with Brashear this afternoon?" she asked suddenly, wanting to hear their supervisor's name spoken aloud, needing the reminder that this was all part of the job.

Sam had just turned to a new page of the sports section. In response to her abrupt question, he went very still for a moment. And then he closed the newspaper. "Yeah," he said. "I'd almost forgotten. Uh, thanks for reminding me."

He didn't sound particularly grateful.

"Maybe I'll try to talk to Polly again while you're gone. I still think she's our best chance at breaking this case. I don't know about you, but I wouldn't mind getting out of this rathole soon."

Sam was looking at her with an odd, shuttered expression far different from the relaxed smile he'd been wearing all morning. Dallas almost regretted bringing up the assignment. For a few wonderful hours, Sam had seemed...well, almost happy. Now he looked more like the man she'd known during the past year—distant, cool, emotionless.

She missed his smile.

He set the paper aside. "I think I'll take a shower and change before I go out."

"Sure," she murmured, and turned nonchalantly back to her paper. As though she wasn't aware that something had just changed between them. Something very important.

SAM LEFT THE APARTMENT at just after four that afternoon. "I'm not sure when I'll be back," he warned. "I'll talk to Brashear, then hang out around the neighborhood for a while. See if I can pick anything up."

"No reason for you to rush back," she said casually. "Maybe Brashear has a new lead for us."

"Yeah. Maybe." He hesitated at the door, shifting his weight from one foot to the other.

Dallas stood beside him, her bulky harness back in place beneath a blue, peasant-style maternity top with a large ruffled collar that kept tickling her chin. She smoothed the collar down for the dozenth time. It gave her something to do with her hands, other than reaching out to cling to Sam. "Watch your back, Perry," she said offhandedly.

He lifted an eyebrow. "Isn't that what you always say to your buddy Pennington?"

"Yeah," she admitted. "Seemed appropriate."

He nodded. "Okay. Keep your guard up, Sanders." He brushed his lips across her cheek, then let himself out.

Her fingertips pressed to the spot he'd kissed, Dallas stared thoughtfully at the closed door. *Keep your guard up.* Brenda's habitual response to Dallas's routine warning.

Apparently, Sam had been watching Dallas more closely than she'd realized during the past months. Did that mean he'd been interested in her even before this assignment had begun? Or did it just mean he was the observant type? Maybe it didn't mean anything at all. Maybe she was just wasting time looking for a faint, tentative reason to hope this wasn't just a convenient, temporary affair.

She closed her eyes and took a long, deep breath. Someone was going to get hurt on this assignment, she thought glumly. It would probably be her. And potential physical danger was the least of her worries.

8

SAM HAD BEEN GONE FOR about an hour when Dallas crossed the hallway and tapped quietly on Polly's door. "It's Dallas," she said, identifying herself in answer to a muffled question from the other side of the door.

Polly opened the door a moment later. She quickly searched Dallas's face. "Anything wrong?"

"No. I just wondered if you'd like to come over and have a cup of coffee with me. I owe you one."

Polly glanced across the hallway toward Dallas's apartment. "Your man home?"

"He's gone out for a while. I don't know when he'll be back." Dallas tried to look wistful and lonely.

Polly took a step backward. "Why don't you come on in here? I don't want to be at your place if he gets home early. He don't much like me."

Dallas looked hesitant. "I . . . uh . . ."

"You're afraid he'll catch you with me?"

"No, of course not," Dallas insisted a bit too quickly. "He doesn't mind if I have friends."

Polly obviously didn't believe her. She stood in the doorway, waiting for Dallas to make her decision. Dallas took a deep breath, glanced both ways down the empty hallway, then pretended to come to a quick decision. "All right. If it's no trouble, I'd love to have a cup of coffee with you."

"Come on in, then. We're letting the cool air out with this door open. What little cool air there is," Polly added disgruntledly. "The air-conditioning in this building sucks."

Dallas commiserated more delicately, waddling into the minimally-furnished apartment behind her pregnant neighbor. She tried to imitate Polly's off-balance posture—not that it was all that difficult to feign, with twenty pounds of padding weighing her down.

SAM SHIFTED THE telephone to his other ear and sipped from the coffee cup he held in his free hand. His sneakered feet were crossed in front of him on his kitchen table, and he slumped comfortably in the big wooden chair. It was nice to be back in his own apartment, in a place where no eight-legged intruders skittered across the floor or counters, where the sounds from outside were nicely muted, where the air was scented with a pine-based air freshener rather than cabbages, onions and human excretions.

Problem was, he missed Dallas. His apartment, where she'd never been, seemed empty now without her.

Real stupid, Perry.

Swiftly and efficiently, he pushed his personal problems aside and completed his report to his lieutenant. "I really don't think anyone on the construction crew knows anything about baby brokers in the neighborhood," he concluded. "I've all but asked outright and haven't even gotten a hint from them."

"So Polly Jones is still our best lead," Brashear said through the phone.

"Yeah. Sanders still isn't convinced Jones is mixed up with them, but I think she is. If anyone can find out for sure, though, it's Dallas," Sam added. "She's already gotten tight with the woman a lot faster than I expected her to."

"Even you have to admit that Sanders is damned good at her job."

Sanders was damned good at a lot of things, Sam could have replied. Instead, he confined himself to a simple, "Yeah. She is."

"So how are the two of you getting along?"

Sam nearly choked on another swig of coffee. He swallowed, wiped his mouth with the back of his hand and casually replied, "Let's just say we've got the neighbors convinced that there's a lot of tension in the Pulaski household."

Brashear chuckled. "I'll bet you do. What? Wait a minute," he said to Sam when a woman's voice spoke in the background. The sound from the other end became muffled, as though Brashear had covered his receiver with his hand.

Sam lifted a curious eyebrow as he waited for his boss to get back to him. As instructed, he'd called Brashear at his home number. So Brashear had a female visitor this afternoon. Interesting. As far as Sam knew, the lieutenant hadn't dated anyone since his wife had died two years ago.

"Hey, Sam?"

He lowered the coffee cup and brought the phone back to his mouth. "Yeah?"

"Pennington says to tell Dallas hello. And she wants to know if the two of you have been picking out baby names."

Sam grinned, though his curiosity had just gone up another notch. What was Brenda Pennington doing at Marty's house this afternoon? Very interesting. "Yeah, as a matter of fact we have. Ask her what she thinks of Bob."

Brashear murmured a question and Brenda replied inaudibly. There was a smile in the lieutenant's voice when he spoke again to Sam. "She doesn't think much of it," he said. "She thinks you can come up with something more original. Like Mathias. Or Reinhold."

Sam sighed gustily. "What ever happened to appreciation for the fine, old, simple names?"

"Like Bob?"

"Right. Or Sam."

"Or Martin. Now *that's* a fine old name."

Sam chuckled. "Bob Martin Perry. Has a nice ring to it. I'll suggest it to Dallas."

"Er—don't you mean Bob Martin Pulaski?"

Sam cleared his throat. "Yeah. Right. That's what I meant to say. Just joking around, all part of the cover story." He was babbling. And, damn it, he thought he might even be blushing. Hell.

"You could be working too hard out in that hot sun, Perry. I think it's time you came in out of the heat, don't you?"

Sam knew what he was being told. His part of the assignment was drawing to an end—or at least, the active role he'd taken thus far. Now it was time for step two. Time for Dallas to take over. It was a good plan, and he knew she could handle it. But he wasn't particularly enthusiastic when he said, "Yeah, I guess it is. I'll check in with you soon as I wrap it up."

"Okay. See you then. Give Sanders my best."

"Sure." Sam hung up the phone, took one last sip of his coffee, then sighed and pushed himself to his feet.

He had a job to do.

DALLAS GIGGLED AT something Polly said, looking across the tiny table with the rather awed admiration she knew Polly found flattering. "You're so funny," she said.

Polly preened. "People say I got a good sense of humor," she admitted, fluffing her lacquered black hair.

"You really do. Your baby's going to have a wonderful time with you for a mother," Dallas dared, watching for a reaction through her lowered lashes.

She got even more of a reaction than she'd expected. Polly's smile vanished and her dark eyes went flat and dull, all the life and sparkle leaving them. Her face seemed to age several years in an instant. "You want some more coffee?" she asked abruptly, effectively changing the subject.

"I'd better get home," Dallas said with a faint sigh, knowing Polly wouldn't say anything more about the baby. For now, anyway. "Sam will be back soon. If I'm not home, he'll be mad—er, I mean, he'll be worried," she corrected herself hastily.

Polly shook her head. "Why do you put up with that jerk?"

Dallas widened her eyes. "I love him," she said fervently, then mentally winced at the breathless sincerity in her voice. Okay, so she was a good actress. So good she'd almost convinced herself. But there was no need to get carried away with this thing, she warned herself sternly.

Polly snorted indelicately. "Love," she muttered. "The word makes me sick. Nothing turns a woman into a spineless victim faster than thinking she's 'in love.'"

"Haven't you ever loved anyone, Polly?" Dallas asked ingenuously.

Polly blew a sharp breath out her nose and raised a hand to the scar on her cheek. She dropped it almost immediately.

Dallas wondered if the gesture had been involuntary.

Before Polly could answer Dallas's question, they were both startled by a heavy pounding on the door.

"Dallas!" Sam's voice roared from the hallway. "Are you in there?"

Dallas drew in a quick, frightened breath. "It's Sam," she whispered unnecessarily.

"That does it," Polly said, slapping a hand down on the tabletop. "I'll be damned if I'm letting him come hammering on my door like that. I've got friends who'll make him wish he weren't never born. They're gonna start with his balls and work their way outward. Nobody, but nobody, uses his fists on my door!" She was already headed for the living room, her voice getting louder with each word, her swollen body quivering with outrage.

Dallas hurried after her would-be champion. "Polly, no!" she said, pleadingly. "I'll handle him. You'll only make him angry if you start threatening him."

Polly tossed a scornful look over her shoulder. "You think I'm scared of *him*? I got friends that make him look like an underdeveloped kindergartener."

Dallas had to admire the woman's nerve. Knowing full well that Polly didn't have any big friends, she still found herself almost believing that Polly was perfectly capable of taking care of one enraged male. "I don't want Sam hurt," she said, quickly trying another tactic. "Please, let me handle this."

Polly grudgingly stood aside as Dallas opened the door, right in the middle of another series of blows. Sam nearly stumbled through the doorway. Dallas would have found it quite amusing if he'd landed on his nose, but he managed to steady himself with one hand on the doorframe. "What the hell are you doing over here?" he bellowed.

"We were just having coffee," Dallas assured him in the meek "little-woman" voice she'd adopted for this role. "I was just coming home to start dinner. Anything you want."

"Get your butt home," Sam said viciously, reaching out to grab her arm and all but drag her into the hallway. He made the motion look realistic enough that Dallas knew she would have marks on her arm where he'd taken hold of her. Not that she blamed him, of course. He was just doing his job.

"Hey, you get your hands off her," Polly said, lurching forward.

Sam stopped her with a finger poked in her shoulder. "You," he said, his voice laced with distaste, "stay away from my woman, you hear? I don't want her hanging out with the likes of you."

"But, Sam, we were just talking about our babies," Dallas lied, looking at Polly to back her up. "We're due at about the same time, and—"

"I don't want to hear about her bastard kid. Or yours," Sam added cuttingly.

Dallas gasped, wilted, and allowed her eyes to fill with huge, pitiful tears. It was a talent she was quite proud of, actually. She could cry at the drop of a hat when she wanted to. It was only when she really needed to that Dallas was usually unable to shed a tear.

"Hey," Polly said, sounding a bit appalled, herself. "That was uncalled for. Ain't no need to hurt her like that."

"You keep your nose out of our business. I'm warning you," Sam added, then reached out and gave Dallas another less-than-gentle shove in the direction of their apartment.

"I got friends, you know," Polly called after them. "*Big* friends," she added loudly, just as Sam slammed their door closed behind himself and Dallas.

Dallas stood in the middle of the living room, unmoving, her head cocked as she listened. A moment later, Polly's door slammed with enough force to rattle their own. She blew out a breath and made a show of mopping her brow. "Whew! *That* was certainly interesting."

"You don't think I overdid it, do you?" Sam asked, frowning.

She shook her head. "You did just fine. You play the jerk very well, Perry. Must be a natural talent."

He didn't smile at the tentative joke. Instead, he reached out, took her hand and examined her arm. "Did I hurt you when I grabbed you back there? I wanted it to look real, but I didn't want to hurt you."

She shook her head again. "You didn't hurt me, Sam," she assured him. "I thought it came off very well."

He was frowning at the faint red marks on her inner arm. He traced them with one finger, then bent his head and touched them quickly with his mouth before stepping back. "If I ever find you with that slut again, I'm gonna beat the living daylights out of you, you got that?" he shouted.

Her arm still tingling from the all-too-brief contact with his lips, Dallas promptly feigned noisy tears and yelled back at him.

The "fight" progressed to more shouts, foot stamping, plate throwing and door slamming before they finally judged it was time for it to end, some two hours after they began.

"Don't want anyone calling the cops," Sam whispered with a faint smile.

Dallas made a rueful face, knowing exactly how most of their neighbors felt about the police.

Tired from their energetic performance, she dropped onto the couch, hitched the harness higher in her lap, and propped her feet on the wobbly coffee table. "So, what did Brashear tell you this afternoon?" she asked, keeping her voice low.

Sam turned on the television for background noise, selected a noisy shoot-'em-up movie, then plopped down beside her. "He says it's time for me to come in out of the sun."

Dallas felt her heart sink, though she'd been expecting this. "You're moving out?"

"No one's going to approach you about the baby if I'm still around. I figured I'll manage to get myself fired from the job tomorrow, then you and I can have another row and I'll move out. You know what to do from there."

"Yes. I'm to grieve myself half sick over you, and blame the baby for coming between us and ruining our beautiful relationship."

Sam nodded. "You got it. If Polly knows anything, she'll tell you."

Dallas thought of the starkly sad look that had crossed Polly's face at the mention of her child. "I think you're right about her, Sam. I think she's already made arrangements to get rid of the baby. I don't know whether she's going through legitimate adoption or selling it, but I don't think she has any intention of raising it."

And Dallas suspected that Polly was already mourning the loss of that child, though the woman hid her pain behind the tough facade she had probably developed years ago.

"Oh, she's selling it," Sam said certainly. "Women like Polly don't give anything away for free."

Dallas sighed, wishing she could disagree; knowing he was right.

"By the way, Pennington said to tell you hi."

Dallas was surprised. "When did you talk to Brenda?"

"I didn't. She was with Marty when I called. She sent the message through him."

"Brenda was at Lieutenant Brashear's house?"

"Yeah."

"Hmm." *How very interesting,* Dallas silently mused with a faint smile.

"I'm getting kind of hungry. Any of that spaghetti left from lunch?"

"Yes. Or I can make something else if you like."

He shook his head. "Leftovers are fine with me. I'll start warming it up."

Dallas looked thoughtfully after him when he left the room. Sam was acting rather strangely this evening. She wondered why he seemed to have erected an invisible barrier between them, when they'd been so close only hours earlier.

Was he preparing himself to leave? Or was he subtly signaling that the affair was coming to an end, along with his part of the assignment?

She bit her lip and concentrated on the action movie unfolding on the fuzzy television screen. It helped her take her mind off the drama unfolding in the tiny, shabby apartment.

SAM'S EMOTIONAL DISTANCE continued throughout the evening. Dallas climbed into bed beside him in a state of uncertainty. Should she turn to him, as she had the past two nights? Should she ask him if anything was wrong? Or should she leave the first move up to him?

For once, the apartment above them was silent. Ms. Oh-my-God-yes! must be out for the evening, Dallas thought as she settled into her pillow. Thank goodness. She really wasn't in the mood to be an unwilling audience to someone else's sexual escapades tonight.

Sam cleared his throat. The sound was so loud in the quiet room, so unexpected, that Dallas jumped.

"Sorry," he said. "Did I startle you?"

"A bit. Er, did Brashear have anything more to say this afternoon?" She couldn't think what else to say at the moment.

"No, not really."

"Oh." She squirmed against the pillow, then asked, "So how are you going to get yourself fired tomorrow?" Not that she particularly cared; she just felt a strong need to make conversation. Anything rather than lie in silence beside him, wondering why he was being so careful not to touch her tonight.

"I dunno. Probably pick a fight with one of the guys or something." He didn't seem particularly interested, either.

"Better make it a small guy," Dallas offered, hoping to make him smile.

"You saying I can't handle a big one, Sanders?" he asked, falling in with her teasing cooperatively enough. But the humor was forced, very different from the laughter they'd shared the day before.

"I don't think I'll touch that line. You make it too easy."

"Someday, Sanders . . ." he growled softly.

She was glad it was too dark for him to see her pathetic attempt at a smile.

She wriggled again on the pillow. Her bare leg brushed Sam's. She jerked away as though she'd been burned.

"What's the matter?" he asked. "Can't get comfortable?"

"No."

"Would a back rub help you relax?"

Relax? With his hands on her? "No!" she said, too quickly.

"Okay, take it easy. It was only a suggestion."

"Sorry. Thanks for the offer."

"Yeah." He lay quietly for another few minutes—long enough that she began to wonder if he'd already fallen asleep. She didn't expect to get a wink of sleep herself; she was too busy wondering what the hell was going on between them.

And then Sam broke the silence again. "Dallas?" His voice was quiet.

"Yes?"

"You seem very far away tonight."

"So do you," she whispered.

His hand touched her shoulder. A moment later she was in his arms, her mouth crushed beneath his.

A LONG TIME LATER, Dallas lay limply against Sam's chest, her body sated, her eyelids heavy. Even as she drifted into a restless sleep, she reflected wistfully that, though they couldn't be any closer physically, Sam still seemed very far away.

Sam was gone when Dallas woke the next morning. Not surprising, since she hadn't slept at all well. It had been sometime around dawn the last time she'd managed to sleep.

Sam had seemed to rest just fine, damn him. He was probably looking forward to getting out of here. Going back to his own clean, comfortable apartment. Going back to work with their friends. Leaving her here alone in this dump, alone in this big, lumpy bed. Damn him.

And then Dallas, who could never cry when it mattered, found that there were real tears rolling steadily down her cheeks. And it suddenly mattered very much.

Sam was back by three that afternoon.

"What are you doing home so early?" Dallas asked clearly when he let himself into the apartment. Just in case anyone was listening.

"I got fired, damn it. And it's all your fault!" Sam yelled.

"*My* fault? How could it possibly be my fault?"

"You kept me up whining at me half the night and I couldn't concentrate on the job today. You're ruining my life!"

Dallas broke into noisy tears again—completely phony tears this time. She was satisfied that Sam would never know she'd shed any real ones over him. "Why don't you just leave me, then?" she wailed loudly.

"Sounds like a hell of a good idea to me!"

"Fine! Then leave."

"Fine! I think I will."

There were more shouts, more noisy sobs, plenty of door banging as Sam shoved his things into a ragged duffel bag. Dallas followed him to the front door, suddenly, shrilly begging him not to go.

"Just shut up! I'm leaving. That's all there is to it."

"Sam, please . . . please . . ."

He hesitated with one hand on the doorknob. Without smiling, Sam Perry looked directly at Dallas Sanders, the roles dropping for a moment. And then he reached out to snag a hand around the back of her neck and pull her to him. The kiss was long, hard, thorough. "Be careful," he whispered when he released her.

"I'll be in touch," she murmured back.

"Do that," he said, then jerked the door open. "Get the hell out of my way!"

"Sam, please . . . please . . . don't go."

"I'm already gone. You know what to do if you want me back," he said with a quick glance at Polly's closed door.

He was just disappearing into the stairwell when Polly's door opened. Dallas broke into noisy, body-shaking sobs.

"What the—" Polly stepped out into the hallway, staring at Dallas, who huddled miserably against the filthy wall. "Hey, are you okay? Did that bastard hit you?"

"He—*left* me," Dallas replied in a rush of heartbroken words. "He's gone, and he said he—he's not c-coming back."

"Look, kid, I'm sorry, but maybe it's for the best, you know?" Polly offered awkwardly. "I mean, he really didn't treat you too good. You got your kid to think about."

Dallas sobbed harder. "I want Sam," she wailed. "I only want Sam. If it wasn't for this baby, I wouldn't have lost him. It's all my fault."

"Your fault? Honey, you're crazy. The kid's half his."

"But he didn't want it. If I—if I'd only been more c-careful," Dallas cried, hiccuping. She mopped at her wet face with the back of one trembling hand. "Now he's broke and out of work and discouraged and I've lost him. I'm all alone. Oh, why did this have to happen to me? Why, why, *why?*"

Careful, Sanders, she warned herself. *Don't overdo it.*

But Polly seemed to be falling for the charade without question. She patted Dallas's shoulder, roughly, self-consciously, obviously uncertain about how to offer comfort. "You'll be okay," she said. "Women like us, we're survivors, kid. We don't need anyone to take care of us. We take care of ourselves, you know? And besides, you ain't all alone. You got friends, you know? Like me."

"I—I have to be alone for a little while," Dallas whimpered, groping for her doorknob. "I have to think about what I can do to get him back. I'll talk to you later, okay, Polly?"

"Yeah, sure, kid. And you just say the word and I'll have my friends track that guy down for you, okay? Maybe they can convince him to do his duty by you, you know what I mean?"

Dallas shook her head, hiding her face behind her hair, as if she were too overcome by emotion to speak. And then she stumbled into her apartment and closed the door behind her, aware that her noisy sobs filtered through the thin barrier.

She ran heavily into the bedroom, as though to throw herself on the bed and dissolve into tears. Only when the bedroom door had slammed behind her did she allow herself to relax. She went into the bathroom to repair the damage her crocodile tears had done to her face. She patted her face with a worn hand-towel, ran a brush through her tangled hair, then walked back into the bedroom. The very empty bedroom. The very quiet bedroom.

She sighed, her gaze focused on the lumpy bed.

She really was going to miss Sam.

9

"GIRL, YOU LOOK LIKE hell. You are going to have to start taking better care of yourself."

Dallas sighed dispiritedly in response to Polly's critical words. She knew exactly how she looked. Like hell, just as Polly had said. And it wasn't all pretense, damn it.

It was Thursday, three days after Sam's dramatic departure. Dallas couldn't believe how much she'd missed him. The apartment had seemed smaller, dirtier, grimmer, uglier since he'd left it. Only by concentrating intently on her job had she been able to keep herself from climbing the grungy walls.

It hadn't been hard for Dallas to pretend that she'd lost her appetite, and any concern about her appearance. In fact, it had been all too easy.

Polly had become her frequent companion. Dallas had sensed the other woman's loneliness from the beginning, but now she knew that Polly had craved companionship. Those "big friends" she'd bragged about had been conspicuously absent during the two weeks Dallas had known her.

"Come on, eat a little somethin'," Polly urged, motioning toward the fast-food feast she'd brought with her to Dallas's apartment a few minutes earlier. "You need to keep up your health."

Even had it not been for the role she was playing, Dallas wouldn't have had the heart to point out that the selection Polly had provided was not exactly healthy for a supposedly pregnant woman. Basically, the menu consisted of deep-fried fats and cholesterol, with a side order of empty calories. But the concern in Polly's dark eyes was genuine, and the gesture had been well-intentioned. Dallas made an effort to eat a few bites, silently grateful that she didn't really have a delicate stomach to contend with.

"That's better," Polly said, watching Dallas swallow a soggy french fry. "You're eating for two, you know."

And consuming enough fat for six, Dallas thought, but managed a weak smile. "This is really good, Polly, but I'm just not very hungry. It was so sweet of you to think of me."

Polly flushed faintly beneath the layer of paint she habitually wore. "Hey, don't start getting all mushy about it," she bluffed, reaching for her own half-eaten double bacon cheeseburger. "I was hungry and I wasn't in the mood to eat alone tonight. Thought you might want to join me."

"Whatever the reason, it was still nice of you," Dallas replied, sincerely this time. "But I won't embarrass you."

Polly shrugged and took an enormous bite of her burger. Her mouth still full, she asked, "You hear from Sam?"

Dallas allowed her lower lip to tremble. Just a little. "No," she murmured, and sighed. "Not a word."

And she hadn't, either. Not that she'd expected to, of course.

She wondered if he missed her. She wondered if he was having trouble sleeping alone. But most of all, she wondered if he *was* sleeping alone.

"Yo, Dallas."

Dallas blinked and looked across the table, finding Polly looking at her strangely. "Yes?"

"Where you been, girl? I've said your name three times."

Dallas blushed. "Sorry. I was, uh, thinking."

"About him, right?"

She could answer with complete honesty. "Yes. About Sam."

Polly made a sound of disgust and shook her head. "Man, you really got it bad. Way he treated you, you'd think you'd be glad to get rid of him."

Trembling lower lip again. A heavy sweep of eyelashes as accompaniment this time. "No," Dallas said on a long, miserable exhale. "I miss him, Polly. I want him back." *Damn it.*

"Even if it means giving up your kid?" Polly asked bluntly.

Dallas rested a hand on the harness and her breath caught in what might have been a sob. "I think so," she whispered. "I can't raise it alone. And I don't want to try without Sam."

"You could give it up for adoption," Polly suggested, avoiding Dallas's gaze as she seemed to concentrate on scooping up a tablespoon of catsup with half a limp fry.

"I know. I wish I thought that would help."

"It would get the kid out of your way."

"But it wouldn't help us financially. That's what Sam's so upset about. He doesn't like to be broke. He's real proud when it comes to money. But I was sick a lot at first and the doctor bills just cleaned us out. Giving the baby up for adoption would mean that I wouldn't have to pay hospital or delivery fees, but it wouldn't replace everything I've already cost poor Sam."

"'Poor Sam,'" Polly repeated, her voice all but dripping with scorn. "Sometimes you just make me sick."

"I'm sorry," Dallas murmured and huddled into herself, looking utterly miserable.

"Oh, hell, now you're doing it with me!"

"Doing what?"

"Letting me treat you like a victim. You ain't no doormat, Dallas. Get up off the floor and quit inviting folks to wipe their feet on you."

Dallas lifted her chin, carefully hiding her amusement at Polly's sharp advice. "Well, what *should* I do?" she asked, allowing herself to show some asperity. "You seem to have all the answers—how are *you* going to support your baby all alone? You don't even have a job."

Polly nodded, seemingly more comfortable with Dallas's aggression than her former meekness. "I got plans," she said simply.

"What plans?"

Polly shrugged. "That's my business."

Patience, Sanders. "Great," she muttered. "You sit there telling me everything I shouldn't do, but you won't give me any advice about what I should do. You won't even tell me what you're going to do."

Polly looked torn for a moment. And then she set the last of her sandwich on the paper plate in front of her and leaned forward, as though concerned that someone else might hear them. "I'm not raising this kid," she admitted. "I'm giving it up."

"Adoption?" Dallas asked, trying to look sad. "Are you sure you want to do that?"

"Look, you're right about one thing. It's damned hard to raise a kid alone, and I want this one to have a better life than I could give it by myself. But I'm not going to end up broke and alone after I have it, like you'll be if you ain't careful."

"Well," Dallas dared, "you won't have a lot of medical bills, probably, but you'll still be broke. You still won't have a job."

"I can get a job anytime I want," Polly returned sharply. "As a matter of fact, I had a high-paying career before I got in this shape, thanks to the latex industry's shoddy workmanship. I could go back to it any time I wanted. But it ain't going to be necessary. I'm getting paid for this kid. Well paid. And I'm taking that money and starting over somewhere nice. Somewhere cool," she added, plucking discontentedly at her sticky maternity T-shirt. "Michigan, maybe. I had an aunt who lived in Michigan. She said it was real pretty there."

"It's real cold there," Dallas said. "Snow up to your chin in the wintertime."

"Beats the hell out of frying eggs on your chin down here in the summertime," Polly retorted with a grin.

Dallas picked at her food, making a small mountain of mangled fries. "So, uh . . . what's this about you getting paid for the kid? You make it sound like you're—well, you know. Selling it or something."

Polly shrugged. "Or something."

Dallas widened her eyes. "You can do that? Legally?"

"Hell, no, it ain't legal," Polly muttered with a scowl and another quick look around them. "Not exactly. But a girl's gotta look out for herself. Nobody else gives a rat's ass, I'll tell you that for sure."

"But what about the baby? What will happen to it?"

Polly glanced down at her stomach, then quickly away. "It'll go to a good home," she said quietly. "They promised me that. Wealthy people, who don't want to waste time with all those stupid bureaucratic rules lawyers make up so they can get rich handling private adoptions. There's a waiting list a decade long for available white babies, and there's plenty of people with enough money and enough determination to get around that list. The kid will get a good home. So why shouldn't I get something out of it, too? I'm doing someone a service. I'm the one who's had to carry the kid all this time. I'm the one who's all swollen and aching and bloated. It ain't fair that I have to suffer and some shark lawyer makes the dough, is it?"

"I hadn't really thought of it that way," Dallas said uncertainly.

"Well, think about it. You go back to your Sam with no baby and a fistful of money and you could probably get him back in a snap—though God only knows why you'd want the creep. As for me, I'm taking care of myself. Just like always."

Dallas put her other hand on the harness, as though she were holding her baby protectively. "I don't know if I could do something like that."

Polly shrugged. "Ain't no one making you. It's just a suggestion."

"I really think you should give this some more thought, Polly. It sounds awfully risky to me. What if you get caught? You could go to jail."

"Wouldn't be the first time," Polly grumbled, then sighed. "Don't look at me like that. I'm no murderer or anything."

"I never thought you were," Dallas assured her loyally.

"Man, it's a wonder you've survived as long as you have. You're about as street-smart as a kitten."

Dallas lifted her chin again, letting it thrust out proudly. "I can take care of myself."

"Yeah. Right."

"I can," she insisted.

"Like you've been taking care of yourself the past week?" Polly asked sharply. "Going without food? Moping around over Sam the creep? Bawling your eyes out?"

Dallas lowered her chin. "I'll get him back," she muttered.

"Mmm. Well, if you want to know any more about what I said, you just let me know. But don't you go talking to anyone else about it, you hear? If I find out you've been running your mouth about my business, you're going to be in a truckload of trouble, you got that?"

Dallas cowered. "You wouldn't turn your big friends on me, would you?"

"I just might," Polly countered, searching Dallas's face as though testing her sincerity. Apparently deciding that Dallas was no more than she seemed, she relaxed. "But I like you, kid, or I wouldn't have said nothing. You won't talk to anybody, will you?"

"Who would I tell?" Dallas asked with a weary smile.

Polly seemed to accept that. "Just don't tell no one."

Dallas ate another lard-dripping fry to avoid answering.

DALLAS COULDN'T BELIEVE her hand was shaking when she raised it to knock on the door in front of her. She couldn't remember the last time she'd been this nervous. She wiped her palm on one leg of her polyester slacks and lifted the hand again. This time she made herself tap firmly on the wooden door.

During the minute or so that followed, she wondered just how Sam would greet her. Professionally— partner to partner? This was, after all, a scheduled working visit. Would he kiss her? Or would he go back to the same brusque, strictly-business manner they'd used before this assignment had begun? Was their affair over, as far as Sam was concerned? Or had he even considered the possibility that it could last for a while? Maybe a long while, if they worked hard enough at it. Dallas was willing; she just wished she knew how Sam felt about it.

He opened the door, and his shuttered expression didn't give her a clue how he felt about seeing her after almost a week. He stepped back to allow her to enter. "Hi. Come on in."

"Thanks." She moved past him, trying not to waddle—which wasn't easy, since she was wearing the harness. She looked curiously around the living room of Sam's apartment, which she'd never visited before. It was nice. Neat, clean, decorated in comfortably overstuffed furnishings in burgundy and green. It wouldn't have been featured in any decorating magazine, but Dallas imagined it was a pleasant place to come home to after a hard day's work.

Sam closed the door and turned to face her. He seemed to grope for something to say, and then he glanced down at her middle and apparently decided to keep it light. "How's Bob?"

She managed a smile. "We're getting by."

"That's good."

"Yeah." She wiped her palms down her pant legs again. "Uh, how have you been?"

He shrugged. "Okay. Been tying up the paperwork on the Perkins case. You know how I hate paperwork."

"Don't we all." This was ridiculous. She felt as though she were on a blind date—and it wasn't going very well. She cleared her throat. "I have a lot to tell you. Polly and I have been talking, and—"

He forestalled her by raising a hand. "Hold on a minute."

She lifted an eyebrow. "What?"

"You want a soda or something? We could at least sit down before you start giving your report."

She twisted her fingers beneath the bulk of the harness. She didn't really want anything, but maybe it would help them relax if they sat down over cool drinks. "Yeah, a soda sounds good. Thanks."

Sam nodded and took a couple of steps toward a doorway she assumed led to the kitchen. And then he stopped, and turned back to face her. "Dallas?"

She swallowed. "Yes?"

"I've missed you."

Her knees weakened. "I've missed you, too," she whispered, wishing she could read that stern face of his.

"I've missed you *a lot*," he said, his frown deepening.

Thoroughly confused, Dallas began to smile, anyway. "I've missed you, too. A lot," she added, taking a step toward him.

He didn't give her a chance to meet him halfway. He was already there, his arms around her, his mouth moving wildly against hers. The harness was a solid intrusion between them, but Sam ignored it. His hands swept her back, settled on her hips and held her as closely as possible under the circumstances. Her mouth opening eagerly beneath his, Dallas strained to get closer.

Sam reached beneath the hem of her blouse and fumbled with the straps of the harness. A moment later, he tossed the bulky appliance out of the way and pulled Dallas firmly against him. Her now slender body settled snugly, intimately, between his thighs. He was already aroused, she noticed dreamily.

So was she.

She needed to touch him. It had been so long....

His face was hard and warm beneath her palms, his jaw firm, and his cheeks lean, both faintly stubbled. His thick, sandy hair was long enough to completely hide her fingers when she buried them in its depths. It hadn't been trimmed since she'd last seen him.

Beneath his white knit shirt, his broad chest expanded against her with his ragged breathing. She could almost feel his heart racing against hers. His solid thighs cradled her between them, locked her against the erection that strained his jeans, emphasized his need for her. His arms were tight around her; strong, hungry.

He felt as utterly perfect as she had remembered.

"I want... I need..." His voice was hoarse, his words awkward with his impatience. He was already groping for the hem of her blouse.

Dallas murmured soothingly against his mouth. "I know what you want. I need it, too," she whispered, lifting her arms to help him rid her of the blouse. And then she tugged at his shirt.

They caught their breaths simultaneously when her uncovered breasts brushed his bare chest. Murmuring his pleasure, Sam cupped her breasts in his hands and lowered his head to kiss the soft upper curves. And then her hardened nipples. She arched backward to give him better access.

She didn't actually remember lowering herself to the floor—or being lowered. One moment she was on her feet in Sam's arms, the next she was lying beneath him, the remainder of her clothing tangled on the floor around them.

Her short fingernails dug into his shoulders as he moved over her, kissing, stroking, nipping, rapidly bringing her to a point of mindless need. She shoved at his jeans, but waited only until he'd opened them and pushed them out of the way before arching demandingly upward. Sam groaned, and buried himself deeply inside her.

SAM'S FACE WAS HIDDEN against her throat, his lips moving very close to her ear. "Dallas?"

She snuggled closer, one hand slowly drifting over his warm, bare back. "Mmm?"

He kissed her earlobe. "How do you like my apartment?"

She giggled. "I like the living room. The carpet is especially nice. Soft, comfortable."

He moved his head to kiss a smile against her slightly tender lips. "If you think the carpet is comfortable, you should try my bed."

"I'll have to do that sometime."

"Yeah. Soon." He kissed her again.

"Very soon," Dallas whispered, her hand sliding to the back of his neck, as she raised her lips to his again.

He groaned and lifted his head. "You have to get back to the apartment soon. And you haven't even told me what you've learned this week."

Dallas lifted an eyebrow and glanced downward. She was completely nude, and tangled intimately with Sam, who had finally kicked off his jeans so that he, too, was unselfconsciously naked. "You haven't exactly given me a chance to report," she told him.

He grinned. "No. I suppose I haven't. Any complaints?"

"Not a one," she assured him.

"Good." He kissed her one more time, then reluctantly drew away. "The bathroom's through that door, if you'd like to, um, freshen up."

She smiled. "Thanks. I believe I will."

"Want me to pour you that soda now? Make some coffee, maybe?"

"Soda's fine. I'll be right back."

The bathroom was done in the same greens and burgundy as the living room. Idly studying the tasteful Paisley wallpaper, Dallas wondered if Sam had decorated it himself. She opened a drawer in search of a comb and swallowed hard when she discovered a tube of lipstick, a pink plastic disposable razor, and a half-empty tube of jasmine-scented bath gel. *Paula,* she thought, quickly closing the drawer.

Had Sam made love to her on that soft living-room carpet?

Dallas scowled into the mirror and combed her hair with her fingers.

Wearing only his jeans, Sam was in the kitchen pouring soda over ice when she rejoined him. A plate of cookies lay nearby—bakery cookies, she noted, wondering if he'd bought them with her visit in mind.

He looked up with a smile. "I thought you might like a snack."

"You know I always like a snack—especially when it's cookies," she replied, reaching for one.

"Yes, I remembered." Leaving the sodas on the table, he walked up behind her and circled her waist with his arms. The maternity top was baggy around her without the harness to fill it in. Sam didn't seem to notice as he held her close and pressed a kiss on the back of her ear. "As cute as you look wearing Bob, it's much easier to hold you this way," he murmured.

"Don't call me cute, Perry," she retorted, finding reassurance in the teasing. "And we are *not* naming the kid Bob. Got that?"

"Not if it's a girl," he agreed. "I was thinking of Bobbie for a girl."

She groaned and rolled her eyes.

Chuckling, he released her, and motioned her to have a seat at the table. "We'd better get work out of the way, I suppose. Marty's going to be wanting a report from me."

Dallas took a seat, drew her soda and the plate of cookies in front of her, and told him everything Polly had said in their revealing conversation the day before.

"I told you she was selling it," Sam said when Dallas finished.

She sighed. "Yes, I know you did. So you get a gold star on your report card. That still doesn't lead us to her contact."

"I think Blivens is involved."

"So do I," Dallas affirmed, remembering the landlady's nosy questions about the state of her health. "But I doubt very much that she's the brains behind the operation."

"I wouldn't say Blivens was the brains behind *any* operation."

Dallas smiled at his dry remark, but let it pass. "I told Polly I'd consider her advice. I'm going to ask to meet her contacts, as though I'm trying to reassure myself about them, but I don't want to push for too much at once."

"You'll let me know when you set up the meeting," he said, and it wasn't a question. "I don't want you meeting them without some sort of backup. Never know when something like this will turn ugly."

They had already agreed upon several ways for Dallas to contact Sam when needed. Remembering them, Dallas nodded. "I'll keep in touch."

Sam suddenly smiled. "So Polly thinks you're crazy to want me back, hmm?"

"Yeah. Totally nuts."

His gaze held hers across the table, and though he was still smiling, his voice suddenly grew more serious. "She's probably right."

Dallas shrugged, without looking away from him. "Maybe. But there it is."

"It's a long way from being over, isn't it, Sanders?" he asked lightly, and she knew he wasn't talking about the assignment now.

She smiled in response to the touch of fear in his expression. She knew the feeling all too well. "No, it isn't over. Not by a long shot."

He ran a hand through his hair. "I didn't expect this," he admitted.

"Neither did I."

"I didn't even want it," he confessed, after clearing his throat.

"Neither did I," she repeated.

"So what are we going to do about it?"

"Finish this assignment first," she said firmly.

He paused for a moment, looking thoughtful, then nodded. "Yeah. You're right, of course."

She spread her hands, as though acknowledging something everyone would know. "Of course."

He made a face and tossed a paper napkin at her.

She laughed and fended it off.

They talked business another fifteen minutes or so, and then Dallas glanced at her watch. "I'd better get back. Polly might start wondering where I am."

"Yeah. Damn, I hate to think about you going back to that pit."

"I'm not exactly looking forward to it, myself," she assured him, grimacing at the contrast between his clean, cozy kitchen and the dump where she would eat her dinner later. "Mind if I see the rest of your apartment first?" she asked impulsively. "I'm curious."

He shrugged. "Sure. C'mon, I'll give you a tour."

Dallas quickly discovered that Sam was quite neat in his home. Remembering how he'd complained about cleaning the apartment, she quizzed him about it. "I didn't see any need for wasting time on that slum," he explained. "It's only a temporary place to stay, and no amount of cleaning is going to improve it much. Why wear yourself out on a useless effort?"

"I told you," she replied. "If I'm going to have to live there, even temporarily, I want it to be as clean as I can make it. I don't like living in filth."

"So we have something in common. We like our homes to be neat."

"We have quite a bit in common, actually," she said seriously, crossing the living room at his side. "We like rock music and action movies, good food and good books. We're both damned good at our job."

"Is this the same woman who recently listed all the reasons we were too different to get involved? You mentioned something about me being a grouch and you an optimist. . . ."

"And I pointed out that you considered me a pain in the butt," Dallas added with a grin. "You agreed, as I remember."

"Yeah," he said, looping an arm around her shoulders. "I still think you're a pain in the butt. But I still like you, anyway."

Like? Dallas wasn't entirely satisfied with the word, but decided it would do for a start. She looked around Sam's bedroom, furnished in English style, with glossy mahogany furniture, hunting prints on the walls, a green-and-burgundy plaid comforter with green pillow shams. It was masculine, yet still warm and inviting. Had Paula decorated it for him?

Dallas swallowed a sigh and chided herself impatiently for dwelling on Sam's former girlfriend. She hadn't come to him a virgin, had fancied herself in love a couple of times before him, but he didn't seem to be obsessing about her past, the way she was his.

She thought the real problem might be that there was still some part of Sam she didn't know; some dark, hidden pain she needed to understand before their relationship progressed much further. She wasn't convinced that it had anything to do with Paula, but she hadn't ruled it out, either. She only knew that the need to understand him was growing stronger, more urgent with each passing moment.

It was no longer possible for her to deny that she loved him. And that knowledge terrified her. If there was any hope that this affair wouldn't end in heart-break, she needed to know everything there was to learn about the enigmatic Sam Perry.

10

SAM LED HER OUT of the bedroom after they reluctantly agreed that there wasn't time for her to test his bed—with him, of course. Dallas motioned to a closed door across the short hallway. "What's in there?"

"A second bedroom. I use it for storage."

She was already headed that way.

"There's nothing in there but junk," Sam protested, though he didn't try to detain her.

"One can learn a lot about someone by looking at their junk," Dallas informed him, opening the door. "What secrets are you hiding in here, hmm?"

Sam smiled and shook his head. "No secrets. Just junk," he repeated.

Dallas paused before turning on the light. "If you mind, say so. I won't be offended," she assured him.

He reached around her and turned the light on. "Knock yourself out," he invited her, standing aside.

She chuckled and walked in.

The room was full. No furniture other than a couple of big, stuffed-full bookcases and a desk that overflowed with more books, tax forms, and bills. Sam wasn't nearly as neat in his paperwork as he was in his living habits. She assumed it was because he despised paperwork.

Large pasteboard boxes were stacked in one corner of the small room. "My mom cleaned out her house when she and Dad moved up north a few years back," Sam explained. "She made me take all my old school and college mementos. Sports trophies and ribbons, photographs, yearbooks, textbooks. I think even my old Boy Scout uniform is in there, somewhere."

"Should've known you were a Boy Scout, Perry."

He only smiled.

Three framed photographs rested on top of one of the bookcases full of battered paperbacks. Dallas studied them. One was of Sam in uniform, probably his graduation photo from the academy. Dallas had a similar photo of herself. The difference was, she looked happy in hers. Sam had worn little expression at all.

A second photograph showed a little boy of about six standing between two adults—a slender, blond woman and a dark-haired man in a police officer's uniform. Sam and his parents, Dallas realized, smiling at the face of a much younger and more innocent Sam. He'd been laughing in the photo. He looked happy. When had he started to change into the more serious, often-troubled man she had somehow managed to fall in love with?

The final photograph, obviously taken several years later, was also of Sam's parents. His mother had aged well, was still slender and blond, though her face was more lined in this picture. His father had grayed and added a few pounds. He was sitting in a wheelchair, his wife standing just behind him with one hand resting on his shoulder. Sam hadn't mentioned that his father was disabled, Dallas mused, wondering how it had happened and whether now was the right time to ask questions.

Still curious, she turned to study the titles in the huge pile of textbooks stacked in one corner next to the bookshelf. They must have been from his college days, she decided, noting that most of them were science courses. And then she realized that the largest number of them had to do with medicine. "What was your major in college?" she asked, glancing over her shoulder at him.

He looked rather uncomfortable when he answered, "Premed."

Her eyes widened in surprise. She'd assumed he'd majored in criminal justice or political science—something having a relation to police work. She certainly hadn't expected this. "You were studying to be a doctor?"

"Yeah." Just one offhanded syllable—yet the deep, old longing in his voice made her heart break.

She turned to face him, realizing that she had just stumbled onto the secret she'd been digging for. "How far did you get with your studies?"

"I'd just been accepted to medical school when I quit to join the police force."

He had been accepted to medical school. He'd been so very close. "What made you change your mind?"

"I didn't exactly change my mind," he answered, avoiding her eyes by halfheartedly straightening some of the papers on his desk. "I had it changed for me. My dad was shot in the line of duty. He walked into a liquor store and was hit by three slugs from a guy who'd just cleaned out the register. He almost died."

Dallas winced. The worst nightmare of every cop and his family. "I'm sorry. It must have been very hard for you and your mother."

"It was hell," he said simply. "Dad was in the hospital for months, and in therapy for several years. The insurance ran out long before the treatments did. His disability payments paid for their necessities, but their savings were gone. We even had to sell their home. I went to work to help out as much as I could."

"You became a cop."

"I had connections," he said with a shrug. "I knew it wouldn't take me long to move into a decent-paying position."

"You couldn't afford medical school?" she asked sympathetically.

"Not if I was going to help my parents. Even before Dad was shot it would have been tight. Medical training costs a fortune. My parents had planned to help as much as they could, but . . . well."

He shrugged, knowing there was nothing left to say.

Sam had dreamed of becoming a doctor. He had never wanted to be a police officer. Dallas was stunned. "I had no idea," she murmured.

"How could you? It's not something I talk about. Plans change. Life goes on. It happens to everyone."

She hated his cool, flippant tone. It didn't disguise the old pain, the still-bitter disappointment. It bothered her that he even tried to hide those feelings from her. "Didn't your parents try to talk you out of quitting school?" she asked.

"They didn't ask me to do it," he answered carefully. "Mom was sort of upset about it, but Dad had always wanted me to follow in his footsteps."

"I would have thought they'd have been very proud if you'd become a doctor."

"I'm sure they would have. But they were very proud when I graduated from the police academy."

"Did you talk about this with Paula?" she heard herself asking, and then mentally kicked herself for not trying harder to resist the impulse. She couldn't help wondering, though, if Paula had approved the decision Sam had made—or resented it.

Sam's eyes narrowed, as though he wondered why she'd asked. "It never came up."

He had lived with the woman—but he'd never shared his old dreams with her? Dallas shook her head. "You really have been alone, haven't you?" she said.

He shrugged and half turned away. "I don't know what you mean."

"Why didn't you go back to school? After your parents were taken care of. Why aren't you going now, if that's what you want so badly?"

He exhaled through his nose, sounding impatient. "By the time my parents were on their feet financially, I was in my late twenties and already established in my job. I've been a cop for nine years, Dallas—since I was twenty-one. I couldn't just quit my job and go back to school. I certainly can't do so now."

"Why not?" she insisted.

"Money, for one thing. It still costs a fortune. I still don't have a fortune."

"There are loans, scholarships, part-time jobs."

"Yeah, right. And by the time I finally worked my way through medical training, I would be forty. Or older. With a mountain of debts to repay."

"Maybe. So?"

He looked at her in disbelief. "Forty, Dallas. Don't you think that's a little old to begin a new career?"

"No. It happens all the time. You're going to be forty, anyway, unless some sleazoid puts a slug in you sometime," she said, deliberately blunt. "You might as well be doing something you enjoy. Even if you start at forty, you'd still have a good twenty years of practice ahead of you—heck, even if for some reason you were only able to practice for a year or two, it would still be worth it if that's what you really want to do. Life is short, Perry. I believe in making every day count."

"Nice little fairy tale, Sanders. Real life doesn't work that way."

"No?" Annoyed now, she moved in front of him, standing so close that he had no choice but to look at her. How dare he speak so condescendingly to her? She knew all too well how life worked—and maybe it was time Sam realized that.

"Look at *me*, Sam. I'm doing exactly what I always wanted to do, from the time I was old enough to watch 'Miami Vice' on TV. Everyone told me it would never happen. I was an abandoned kid who grew up in orphanages and generally lousy foster homes. I was sexually molested by a foster-care worker when I was ten, busted for shoplifting with a group of rebel friends when I was twelve, and had experimented with several illegal substances and alcoholic beverages by the time I was sixteen."

Chin held high, she continued without giving him a chance to verbally react to any of her revelations, though she watched the expressions flashing across his face. "I was angry and stubborn and defiant and fiercely independent. More than one social worker predicted that I'd end up dead or working the streets like Polly. But when the time came for me to get out on my own, to decide what I wanted to be, I knew they were wrong. No one was going to tell me I couldn't be whatever I wanted—and I wanted to be a cop. It took a lot of work, more than a few confrontations with those who would have held me back, but I made it, Sam. And I love it."

He'd gone rather pale during her impassioned speech, especially when she'd admitted that she'd been abused as a child. His hand wasn't quite steady when it touched her cheek. "I know you love your work, Dallas. I've always envied you that."

"So what are you going to do, sit around being jealous of me for the rest of your career? Spend another thirty-five years in a job you've never liked?" she challenged, holding his eyes with her own. "Or are you going to do something about getting what *you* want?"

"Dallas, this is ridiculous. I can't go back to medical school at this point in my life. I haven't even considered it."

"That's a lie," she said evenly.

He flushed. "Okay, I've thought about it. But I've never seriously considered it."

"Then you're a coward."

He scowled. "Now wait a minute—"

Still peeved at the way he'd brushed her off—or tried to—she was torn between reaching out to take him in her arms, and taking him by the shoulders and shaking him. Hard.

"I want you to be happy, Sam. Don't you see that? You're probably the finest man I've ever known. You gave up your dreams to help your parents, you've performed a job you never really wanted with competence and distinction, you care about the people around you, the people you work with and the ones you've sworn to protect. You deserve to be happy."

He reached out suddenly and pulled her close. "Don't make me out to be some sort of hero, Dallas. It isn't true."

"To me it is," she whispered, clinging to him. She could have told him then that she loved him. She didn't, because she knew he wasn't ready. He had too much to think about already. And she didn't want his decisions for his future influenced by any demands he might imagine her feelings made upon him.

She realized that she was even willing to give him up if it meant that the deep-seated unhappiness in him, which she now understood, could be replaced with contentment. So this was love. It seemed she'd never really known the emotion before, after all. Compared to this, the others had been little more than infatuation.

It hurt, she realized. But she could no more stop loving Sam than she could stop breathing.

"Think about what I said," she murmured, pressing a kiss to his hard cheek. "It's not too late, Sam. It's never too late to go after what you want."

"You're all I want right now," he said gruffly and crushed her mouth beneath his.

Dallas kissed him back with all her heart, but she knew it wasn't enough. As much as she cared for him, it would take more than her love to truly make him happy. How could he ever be content when he was trapped in a career he had never wanted, that he'd found so little joy in? And if Sam wasn't fully happy, could they ever really be happy together?

"I have to go," she said with a sigh, drawing away from him.

"I know." His jaw flexed, a sign of his unwillingness to see her leave. "Be careful."

"I'm always careful, Perry." *Except where you're concerned.*

He walked her to the door. He stopped her just as she reached for the doorknob. "Uh, Sanders?"

She glanced over her shoulder. "Yeah?"

"Aren't you forgetting something?"

She frowned. Her purse was in her hand, so she knew he wasn't referring to that. "Am I?"

He grinned. It always amazed her how his rare, full smiles could transform his dark face.

Sam knelt and retrieved something large and bulky from the floor next to the couch. "Does the name Bob ring a bell?" he asked, dangling the heavy harness from one hand.

Dallas groaned and slapped a hand to her forehead. "Oh, my God, I forgot it." She was genuinely chagrined. In her entire career, she'd never made that kind of monumental mistake while working undercover.

Sam was obviously amused by her embarrassment. "I think Polly might have noticed."

"Yeah," Dallas said grimly, reaching for the harness. "I'm sure she would have."

"Need help getting back into that thing?"

"You start fumbling around under my clothes and it'll be midnight before I leave," Dallas retorted, turning her back to him as she raised her shirt.

"There is that."

She felt him watching with interest as she strapped herself into the rig, then smoothed the maternity shirt back into place. "Now," she said in relief, turning back to him. "How do I look?"

"Beautiful," he assured her, no longer smiling.

She blushed. "That was nice," she said, caught off guard. "Thanks."

"It just happens to be true." He kissed her, but touched her only with his mouth. Dallas suspected he was resisting temptation. She knew how he felt. It was taking all her willpower to keep her hands off him.

"Take care of yourself," he murmured as he stepped back.

She had the door open and was halfway out when she looked back at him. "You'll think about what I said?"

"I'll think about it."

She couldn't read his expression. She didn't waste any more time trying. She left then, while she still could.

SHE CRIED ALL THE WAY back to the apartment. The people on the bus around her looked uncomfortable in the presence of a sobbing pregnant woman, but only one elderly black woman asked if there was anything she could do to help. "No," Dallas whispered miserably. "But thank you."

The woman awkwardly patted Dallas's shoulder. "It'll work out, honey," she offered bracingly. "Whatever it is, you'll find a way to work it out. Just you wait and see."

"Th-thank you," Dallas murmured brokenly, giving the sweet lady a feeble attempt at a smile and feeling a bit guilty about deceiving her this way.

The tears had a purpose, of course. Dallas needed to return to her apartment with a red nose and tear-streaked cheeks in order to reinforce her cover. Again, she was rather pleased with her acting talents. Had she not chosen a career in law enforcement, she probably could have made a living on the big screen, she decided.

Which only made it easier for her to cry as she thought of how Sam had abandoned his own career dreams. She hoped his parents were properly grateful for the sacrifice he had made for them. She suspected they didn't fully realize what Sam had given up.

Dallas understood all too well. She knew what it was like to have a dream. Knew what it felt like to be on the verge of letting it go. Knew how it was to be the only one who believed in that dream.

No wonder Sam had become such a loner. He hadn't believed there was anyone who truly understood. She could identify with that, too.

She loved him. She wanted him to have everything he'd ever wanted—even if it meant pushing him away, freeing him to go after his dreams.

Her tears weren't all feigned by the time she stepped heavily off the bus and made her way toward the joyless apartment building.

SAM STARED AT THE battered copy of *Gray's Anatomy* he held in his left hand. *Medical school,* he thought scornfully. At his age? Dallas must have temporarily lost her mind to even suggest such a thing.

He couldn't do it, of course. Couldn't walk away from a successful, nine-year career to go back to school now. Even if he could get accepted again—and that was a very big if—it would be too hard. He wasn't sure he even remembered how to study. Medicine was nothing more to him now than a boyhood dream, the way some kids once dreamed of being astronauts or superheroes.

Or cops, he thought, remembering Dallas's words.

Damn, but she'd had a tough life. How could she still be so much of an optimist? How could she possibly believe that life could all come out just the way it should if someone was just willing to work hard enough at it?

She was wrong, of course. Just because it had worked for her, just because she had managed to overcome enormous odds, didn't mean everyone could. Nor that everyone even wanted to try.

It was too late for him.

And even if he should lose his own mind and go back to school, Sam thought, shoving the thick book back onto its shelf, was Dallas aware of how hard that would be on any sort of personal life they might have? He'd be spending long, hard hours studying, working parttime, probably, and then more grueling hours and seemingly endless nights working as an intern and a resident. The real truth was that he wanted it so badly his mouth watered just thinking about it—but would Dallas be able to live with those demands on his time? Assuming she was even considering hanging around that long, of course.

He'd had to make a choice once. Follow his dream, or give it up to help his parents out of a desperate situation. The choice had been painful, but not really difficult. He couldn't have lived with himself had he taken the selfish path then; would have taken no pleasure from any success he might have found.

If he allowed himself to be swayed by Dallas's bold advice—to risk going after that old dream again—would there come a time when he'd have to choose between his dream and Dallas?

He wasn't sure he could survive having his hopes shattered again. But he was equally sure he didn't want to live the rest of his life without Dallas Sanders in it.

He'd once wondered if he was capable of falling deeply, permanently in love with any woman. Now he knew that he was. He'd fallen in love with Dallas Sanders, of all people.

He groaned and rammed his fist against the wall. Why did life always have to be so damned complicated?

POLLY REACTED TO Dallas's tear-ravaged face exactly as Dallas had hoped she would. "What happened?" she gasped, clutching Dallas's arm with one scarlet-taloned hand. "What's wrong?"

"I—I saw Sam," Dallas confessed brokenly. "He—he said he isn't going to change his mind about the baby.

He doesn't want it. He'll never want it. And he doesn't want me if the baby comes with me."

Polly relaxed a bit, though her dark brows drew together in a scowl. "What did you do, go crawling to him? Beg him to take you back?"

Dallas nodded disconsolately. "Yes. It didn't work," she sniffed. "He gave me some money for food and then told me he hadn't changed his mind."

"I could have told you that," Polly muttered. And then she sighed. "Well? What are you going to do?"

Dallas paced her living-room floor, trying to look torn. "I don't want to lose Sam."

"Does that mean you're willing to lose the kid?"

Dallas touched the harness. "It's probably better this way," she whispered. "What kind of life could I give it?"

She turned slowly to Polly. "You're sure these people you told me about find good homes for the babies?"

"Rich homes," Polly said. "People with money and power. The kid wouldn't lack for anything."

Except scruples, Dallas could have retorted. Being raised by wealthy people who didn't hesitate to break the law for their own convenience was hardly an ideal upbringing. She'd seen the kind of people who'd been raised with money and power and no respect for the law or the rights of others. People like that gave no thought to the "little people" left strewn behind them like unidentifiable roadkill.

No child of Dallas's would ever be raised in that atmosphere—and she was going to do her best to make sure that Polly's baby wasn't, either. "I'd like to meet them," she said.

Polly hesitated. "Meet who?" she asked carefully.

"The people you've been talking to. The ones who are going to pay you for your baby. The ones who are going to make sure your baby goes to a good home."

For the first time since Dallas had known her, Polly looked uncertain. "You're sure you want to do this? These people are very serious about this, Dallas. Once you give them your word, they aren't going to let you back out."

Dallas took a deep, shaky breath. "How much will they pay me? After all the hospital expenses, of course."

"Enough to make Sam's eyes light up again," Polly retorted. "But you can't decide something like this on impulse, kid. You gotta think about it."

"Did *you* think about it?"

"I didn't have a whole lot of other options," Polly said bitterly. "The money these people are paying me will let me start a whole new life somewhere. I need that."

"I need to start my life over, too," Dallas insisted. "With Sam."

Polly sighed. "I still think you're crazy. For one thing, I think you got feelings for this kid. I don't think it's going to be easy for you to give it up."

Her hand still on the padding, Dallas tried not to be amused at the unintentional irony. Polly couldn't begin to guess how anxious Dallas was to finish this assignment and permanently rid herself of the hot, heavy harness—so anxious that she'd almost blown everything by forgetting to put it back on before leaving Sam's place!

"I can handle it," she said. "I want to do this, Polly. Please help me."

Coming to an abrupt decision, Polly nodded her dark head. "Okay. Fine. I'll talk to them."

"I'll come with you."

"No." Polly spoke sharply, flatly. "*I'll* talk to them. They don't welcome strangers around much. If they're interested in talking to you, they'll tell me. If not— you're on your own, you got that? One word from you to anyone about this, and you'll be lucky if you live long enough to go into labor."

Dallas gasped. "They're that dangerous?"

"People are always dangerous when enough money is involved," Polly answered matter-of-factly. She searched Dallas's face. "You still want to talk to them?"

Dallas gulped audibly, but nodded. "Yes. I still want to talk to them."

"I'll see what I can do."

"Thank you."

Fifteen minutes later, Dallas was alone. She ran a hand through her hair and gave a weary sigh.

All in all, it had been one hell of a day.

THE MEETING TOOK PLACE on Sunday afternoon. Dallas wasn't surprised that the leader of the baby-selling ring working the neighborhood turned out to be a friend of the surly Ms. Blivens. It seemed that Blivens passed along the occasional tip on a baby-source prospect in exchange for cash. It had been Blivens who'd brought Polly into the scheme.

The woman introduced herself only as Myra, an attorney. She was rail thin, with limp, dark hair and hard, lifeless eyes. Dallas had no doubt that the woman was cunningly intelligent. That became obvious during their brief meeting, when Myra skirted skillfully around any concrete promises and offered only veiled innuendos that were far from providing enough evidence for successful prosecution. With what little she'd said so far, a clever lawyer could make a case that Myra was only offering her services to set up a legal, private adoption.

Dallas knew better.

"I didn't like her," she told Polly later when they were alone in Polly's living room.

Polly shrugged, and pressed a hand to her back as though it ached. "Who said you gotta like her? Her money's good."

"Are you sure we want our babies to go to someone like her? What if she's lying about making sure they'll go to good homes? What if she's selling them to people who'll abuse them or something?"

Dallas saw the anxiety that flashed in Polly's eyes, though it was quickly masked. "She ain't going to do that," she insisted. "Myra says the people wouldn't want babies so bad if they weren't willing to take care of them."

"But what if she's lying?" Dallas insisted.

"Look." Polly spoke sharply, irritably. "She's not, okay? You're the one who nagged at me to set this up. Now you better not start changing your mind."

"Why not? I didn't agree to anything," Dallas protested, crossing her arms over her protruding middle.

"You saw her. You could identify her to the cops."

"Why would I go to the cops? I could get into trouble."

"Yeah, you just remember that."

"Besides, she never really said anything about buying the baby. She hinted, but she never committed. She wouldn't even commit to a firm fee."

"She's not crazy, Dallas. She ain't going to give you more than you need to know at this point."

"How are you going to get your baby to them? Will they pick it up at the hospital?"

"Don't be stupid. I'll bring the kid home. It's gotta look like I'm going to keep it or Child Welfare starts getting involved."

"So you give them the baby later, after you're released from the hospital?"

"Yeah. We'll arrange an exchange point and everything will be taken care of. I'll take my money and disappear. Start over somewhere else with a new name, a new life."

"How do you know you can trust them? How do you know they aren't conning you?" Dallas persisted. And then she gasped as if at a sudden flash of thought. "What if Myra's a cop?"

"A cop?" Polly dropped her hand from her back and gave a snort of laughter. "Yeah, right."

"No, really, Polly. What if she's trying to set you up? You could hand her the baby and she could arrest you. You could go to jail for a long time. Me, too, now. I'm scared."

Polly lifted both hands. "Calm down, you're getting hysterical. Myra ain't no cop, okay? Trust me, I know a cop when I see one."

Dallas looked skeptical. "How?"

"Let's just say I have experience. Myra's a snake, but she's no cop."

"I still say you should think about this some more," Dallas argued.

There was no mistaking the haunted look that crossed Polly's face then. "Maybe you can still change your mind," she said, her voice low. "You haven't really committed yourself. You could disappear now and they wouldn't come looking for you. Probably. But I've made 'em a promise. I've already taken money. Already spent it. I change my mind, they're going to want revenge."

Dallas lifted a hand to her throat. "But—"

"Look, I knew someone, okay? Someone who promised them her kid, then changed her mind after she had it. She turned up in the river a few days later. No one knew for sure what happened to the kid. You think that was a coincidence? I ain't that dumb."

"Oh, Polly. What have you done?" Dallas asked sadly.

Polly lifted her chin. "I'm taking care of myself," she said. "Just like always. And you better be prepared to do the same. I don't see that man of yours around to take care of you."

The faint remnants of fear behind Polly's bravado made Dallas's throat tighten. She still didn't approve of Polly's choices, was still prepared to arrest her if she eventually refused to cooperate with the sting, but she felt rather sorry for her, anyway. Misguided as she'd been, Polly had obviously felt that she'd had no other choices.

Like Sam, Dallas thought with a silent sigh.

She hoped it wasn't too late for either Polly or Sam to turn their lives around. She had grown fond of one, fallen in love with the other. And now she found herself caught right in the middle of their personal dilemmas.

It was a damned unnerving position to be in, she thought ruefully.

11

IT TOOK DALLAS ANOTHER week to break through Polly's brittle defenses and finally discover the woman's true feelings about selling her baby.

It happened almost by accident. They returned home from walking to the grocery store together and found a small package sitting outside Polly's door. Polly bent with difficulty to pick it up. "Wonder what this is?"

Dallas shifted the small bag of groceries she'd just purchased to her other arm. "Come on in for coffee. You can open it at my place, if you want."

Polly nodded, suspiciously examining the brown-paper-wrapped box.

Dallas put away the few supplies she'd purchased and put water on to boil for instant coffee. "You going to open that or stare a hole through it?" she asked Polly, who was still studying the package.

Polly shrugged. "Guess I'll open it." She ripped the paper and tossed it to one side, revealing a small, inch-thick white gift box. She lifted the lid.

Her breath caught audibly. Dallas stepped closer to see what had caused Polly's look of stunned disbelief.

The baby outfit was incredibly soft looking. It was made of white cotton—a one-piece garment suitable for a newborn boy or girl—and was accompanied by little white booties. "It's adorable," Dallas said. "Who's it from?"

With hands that weren't quite steady, Polly plucked a small square card from the box. "It's from Blivens," she said, her voice carefully uninflected. "It says she wanted me to have something for the kid to wear home from the hospital."

"How weird," Dallas said, frowning. "I wouldn't have thought she'd do something like this." It seemed unbelievably cruel, under the circumstances.

Polly shrugged, her dark eyes locked on the tiny outfit still in the box. "I guess she knew I wouldn't think to buy anything. They want the baby to look good to anyone who's interested enough to notice."

"Oh." Dallas reached toward the box. "Mind if I look at it?"

"No, go ahead," Polly said, though Dallas noted she'd stiffened a bit.

Dallas held the little romper up in front of her. "It's so soft," she murmured. "So tiny."

Polly looked away, but not before Dallas had seen the flash of pain that crossed her face. "You'd better put it back in the box," Polly muttered. "Don't want to get it dirty."

Dallas carefully folded the garment and tucked it back into the box. And then she rested a gentle hand on Polly's stiff shoulder. "Polly? You don't really want to give your baby up, do you?" she asked quietly.

"Don't be stupid."

"I'm not being stupid. I'm being a friend. And I can see that you're hurting."

Polly shook her head fiercely, her face still averted. "You're nuts. I never wanted this kid. Certainly didn't plan it. I should have gotten rid of it as soon as I found out about it, but I went temporarily crazy, I guess, and then it was too late. But that don't mean I'm not smart enough to get something out of it."

"You really think you can be happy living on money you received from selling your own child?"

Polly gasped at the question. She stood so fast her chair clattered against the floor. "What the hell—? I thought you said you were my friend!"

"I am," Dallas insisted. "I like you. Quite a bit, actually. And I think you're making a horrible mistake."

Polly reached out for the gift box. "I'm getting out of here," she mumbled. "If you feel like this, there's nothing more for us to say."

"Polly," Dallas said quickly, hoping she hadn't just ruined everything. "I won't say any more about it. *If* you can look at me and tell me without hesitation that it won't tear you apart to hand your baby over to Blivens and Myra."

Polly looked sullen. "I don't have to tell you nothing."

"No. But why shouldn't you tell me—if it's true? Unless you're afraid to admit the real truth?"

Polly jerked her head. "I ain't afraid of nothing."

Dallas didn't respond, just looked at her.

Polly sighed. "You can be a real pain in the butt, Pulaski."

Dallas's lips twitched just a bit. "That's what Sam tells me."

Polly's scowl deepened even further at the comparison to the man she detested. "Okay," she said flatly. "Maybe it won't be so easy giving Myra the baby. I wish the whole thing could be arranged a little different— you know, where I'd never have to see the kid. But this is the way it has to work. And it ain't like I got any other choices, remember?"

"You could keep the baby."

Polly snorted. "Yeah, right. Me, raising a kid? I wouldn't know what to feed it, what to do if it got sick—hell, I couldn't even help it with homework."

"There are people who can help you with all of that."

"I can't be nobody's mother, Dallas," Polly repeated miserably. "You don't understand."

"You think not?"

Polly shook her head. "It's what I am, you see. What I've been. I mean, I'm planning to change everything once I start over in Michigan. Get a real job, maybe. But I can't start over with a baby to worry about."

"Of course you can, if you want."

"How? By going back on the streets? Just the kind of mom the kid needs, right?"

"You don't have to go back on the streets."

Polly shrugged. "You don't understand," she repeated. "Hell, you probably never even met a hooker before."

"What does that have to do with it? I don't have to approve of your past to be your friend now."

Defensive again, Polly crossed her arms over her swollen stomach. "I never asked for your approval. Or nobody else's."

"I know that. It's your life. Your choices. And now you have another choice. You can sell your baby to these people who care more about money than human life—or you can keep it. Raise it. Do something worthwhile with the rest of your life."

For a quick, revealing moment, Polly looked terrified.

"Even if you decide you don't want that responsibility, you can still do the right thing by your child," Dallas persisted. "You can give it to a legitimate adoption agency, people who will carefully screen the potential parents. Who'll make sure that your baby goes to the people who are most qualified to raise it—not to the ones with the most cash available to buy a child."

"You really are naive, aren't you?" Polly whispered. "You believe an ex-hooker can be a good mother—and that so-called legitimate adoption guarantees a happy, safe home for a kid. And you really think Myra's going to stand back and let me change my mind about doing business with her. I guess you're going to tell me there's no way I'd end up floating in the river."

"I'm not quite as naive as you think," Dallas argued, though the words stung a bit, especially since Sam had thrown them at her recently. She wasn't naive—life had seen to that. But was there anything wrong with learning to hope for the best? With being determined to succeed, no matter how hard it might be?

She knew life didn't always work out for the best. In her job, she'd seen the worst it had to offer—and occasionally caught glimpses of the best. She'd seen the rare acts of heroism amid the carnage, had met those few who'd triumphed over seemingly insurmountable odds to make a real difference in the often-ugly world around them. She'd made the conscious decision at the age of eighteen that she wanted to be one of the good guys; one of the ones who tried to make a difference, even if her efforts were thwarted more often than they succeeded. She still had to try.

"I just want you to be happy," she said, busily making plans.

Polly shrugged and looked away. "I'll settle for having enough money to get by for a while," she muttered. "Look, I don't want to talk about this anymore, you hear? Not now, not ever. I'm starting to worry about trying to help you. You ain't careful, you're going to get both of us tossed in the river."

"I'll be careful," Dallas promised.

"Then just keep your mouth shut from now on, okay? You do whatever you want about your kid, and let me take care of mine. If you don't want to deal with Myra, then you'd better disappear. Find another place to stay. It ain't safe for you here."

"Thank you for caring."

Pushed to the edge, Polly rubbed a weary hand at the small of her back and shook her head. "You're too much, Pulaski." She snatched up the box. "See you around."

"Will you still go with me to the clinic in the morning? You promised you would."

Polly grimaced. "I don't know—"

"Please, Polly. I'm afraid of doctors. Sam always went with me before. He didn't like it, either, but he went."

"Oh, hell. All right, I'll go. Damn it, Pulaski, sometimes I wish you'd never shown up around here."

"I know." *And you haven't heard anything, yet,* she could have added, thinking ruefully of her plan for the next day.

Polly left without saying anything else. Dallas knew she'd done all she could to convince Polly of the harmful path she'd set out on.

Now it was up to Polly to decide whether she wanted to willingly cooperate with Dallas's next request.

THE FREE CLINIC WAS A madhouse, as always. Pregnant women crowded into an undersize waiting area, several of them accompanied by small children who ripped through the room, whooping and squealing. Computers hummed, names were shouted, babies screamed from the indignities of examinations or the pain of immunizations. Dallas wondered how the woman working behind the reception desk managed to look so calm and unruffled. "I'm Dallas Pulaski," she said, making sure Polly was close by. "I believe I'm expected."

The woman didn't even blink. "Down the hallway, third door on the left," she said.

Dallas turned to Polly, who looked a bit surprised by the exchange. "You'll come with me, won't you?"

"Into the exam room? C'mon, Dallas, give me a break."

"Please? I really don't want to go in there alone. You're used to this by now."

Polly grimaced and rubbed her stomach. "Yeah, but—"

"Would you rather stay out here? With all this?" Dallas asked, nearly stumbling when a small child barreled into her from behind, leaving sticky handprints on Dallas's maternity jeans.

Polly took one look around and turned back to Dallas. "Okay, I'll come with you. If the doctor don't mind."

"He won't mind," Dallas assured her, and led the way down the hallway. When she reached the third door on the left, she paused, took a deep breath, said a quick, mental prayer and reached for the doorknob. "Okay, here goes."

Dallas motioned Polly to precede her into the room. She followed, closing the door firmly behind her. The room was already occupied; the man stood with his back to the door, apparently absorbed in studying some complex-looking medical equipment arranged on a wall behind the paper-covered exam table. He looked around when they entered.

Polly stiffened, stopping in her tracks.

Dallas swallowed, and mentally crossed her fingers. "Hi, Sam."

He walked around the end of the table, then leaned comfortably against it. "Hi," he said, his watchful eyes never leaving Polly's frowning face. "Hello, Polly."

"What the hell are you doing here?" Polly demanded, and turned to Dallas. "If you knew he was going to be here, what did you want me for?"

"Sam and I want to talk to you, Polly," Dallas said quietly. "It's about your baby. We want to help you. We *can* help you, if you'll let us."

Polly's eyes narrowed—and then suddenly widened. "Oh, hell," she muttered, stumbling back a step. "Oh, damn."

Sam moved quickly, blocking Polly's path to the door.

Dallas reached out, afraid Polly would fall over the stool so close behind her. "Be careful," she warned.

Polly had backed almost against a wall. "You're a cop," she said, her whispered voice dripping with accusation. "You're a goddamned cop."

"I'm afraid so. We both are."

"Oh, hell," Polly said again, her eyes flaming with betrayed fury. "So much for *friendship*."

Dallas winced. "I'd like to think we have become friends, Polly. But I don't blame you for being angry."

"Am I under arrest?"

"You aren't under arrest," Dallas assured her. "You haven't really done anything wrong—not yet. We're here to offer you immunity and assistance. In exchange for your cooperation, of course."

Polly's reply was pithy and succinct.

Dallas sighed. "I figured you'd react that way. At first."

Polly stood like a sullen statue during the next fifteen minutes while Dallas outlined what they wanted her to do in exchange for the immunity they'd promised. Sam wisely stayed out of it, his back against the door, his arms crossed over his chest, certainly aware, as Dallas was, that Polly was more likely to be persuaded by Dallas.

"And if I say no?" Polly demanded.

Dallas looked sympathetic. "Then we spread a few rumors that you've been talking with the police. Even if they have no proof, Myra and her friends can't take the risk that it's true. They'll either disappear—or you will."

"And if I choose to do that, anyway?" Polly challenged. "If I walk out of here and get on a bus to somewhere?"

"You could do that, of course," Dallas admitted. "We can't legally stop you. But you'll only end up alone in a strange town, with a baby due at any time and no one to care about you."

"No one cares about me now," Polly said bitterly. "You only want me to help you bust Myra and Blivens."

It stung, but Dallas didn't try to argue. When it came right down to it, Polly was right, in some ways. If Dallas were forced to choose between her fondness for Polly and her job, she would choose the job. It would sadden her to have to arrest Polly—but she would do it, should it become necessary for any reason. "We can help you," was all she could say. "You and your baby."

Polly touched her stomach. Fleetingly. And then she glanced down at Dallas's middle. "So where did they find a pregnant cop, anyway?" she grumbled.

Dallas smiled. "They didn't," she replied, and lifted the hem of her blouse.

Polly took one look at the harness and swore. Fluently. At length. Dallas waited patiently.

When Polly had vented until she'd run out of breath, Dallas stepped forward. She didn't touch Polly, knew her touch wouldn't be welcome just now, but she tried to express her concern with her eyes, her voice. "You don't want to sell your baby to these people, Polly. We know about people like them—about the ones they do business with. Don't you realize the buyers are usually people who have been turned down by legitimate agencies—for good reason? Do you really want to put your defenseless baby in their hands?"

"I thought I was doing the right thing," Polly muttered, her dark eyes overly bright. "The only thing I knew to do."

"I know. You didn't realize you had any other choice. But you do. You can keep your baby, take advantage of the programs that would help you raise it—or you can make sure it goes to a good home. One that you choose, if you like. You don't have to sell it like a piece of merchandise." *The way you've so often sold yourself,* Dallas could have added, but didn't. The unspoken words hung in the air, anyway.

Polly took a deep breath. "They'll kill me."

"No," Sam said, speaking for the first time since greeting Polly. "They won't hurt you. Not if you're willing to cooperate."

"I've heard of other people who cooperated with the cops and ended up dead."

Sam inclined his head. "It's happened," he admitted. "But it won't this time. For one thing, we're dealing with a small-potatoes organization, here. We've traced this Myra, and she's a storefront attorney who's been investigated more than once for shady business practices. She's probably working with her boyfriend, who's got a record for running scams. Blivens is probably the only other person they've brought in to help them with this. We don't have enough evidence to prosecute any of them, but with your help we can bust them. They don't have enough clout to be any danger to you after that. We'll keep you safe."

"I'd step in front of a bullet myself to keep you and your baby out of danger," Dallas said evenly.

Polly took a quick breath. "Big words," she accused, sounding disbelieving. But Dallas could see that she wasn't entirely unaffected by the rash promise.

"That won't be necessary," Sam said sharply, shooting a frown at Dallas.

She smiled at him. "No. I'm sure it won't." But she'd meant it, anyway, and they both knew it.

Sam might as well know now that she would always perform her job with everything she had. She wouldn't take unnecessary risks; she didn't want to die, even heroically. But the danger would always be there. The last man she'd dated hadn't been able to handle it. She didn't know if Sam's personal experience with the job would make it easier for him to accept the risks—or harder.

Polly was looking from Dallas to Sam, watching the silent exchange between them. "You two really are a couple, aren't you?" she asked curiously.

Dallas cleared her throat and felt her cheeks warm. Sam seemed suddenly fascinated by the array of wrapped tongue depressors and cotton swabs scattered across the countertop beside him. "We, uh, we're partners," Dallas said, then quickly changed the subject. "Are you going to help us?"

"Why should I?" Polly demanded, holding Dallas's gaze.

"For your baby," Dallas replied, risking everything on her instincts about Polly's true nature.

Polly inhaled deeply. "Damn."

Dallas only waited.

Polly finally sighed. "All right, I'll do it," she muttered. "I'll probably end up dead, but I'll do it. It ain't like you two have given me any other choice," she added resentfully.

"You will end up dead if you aren't very careful," Sam warned. "You've got to play this straight, Polly. You've got to watch what you say and how you say it. Blivens and her friends can't even get a hint that anything has changed."

Polly cocked one hip and tossed back her hair. "I know how to run a scam."

"I'm sure you do," Sam murmured, making no effort to hide his amusement.

The look Polly gave him should have singed his hair. Dallas shot him a repressive frown.

Sam held up both hands in surrender. "All right, it's up to you two now. Good luck."

"Something tells me we're going to need it," Polly mumbled.

Dallas silently agreed.

"Am I free to leave now?" Polly asked, her voice still laced with defiant sarcasm, her only pretense at control now that her choices seemed to have been made for her.

"We'll leave together, the way we came in," Dallas answered.

Sam touched her arm. "Polly, would you wait in the reception area for just a few minutes? I need to talk to Dallas, but I'll make it quick."

Polly gave a long-suffering sigh, rolled her eyes, then glanced at her watch. "Ten minutes," she said. "Then I'm out of here, with you or without you," she told Dallas flatly.

Dallas nodded agreement. She waited until Polly had closed the door behind her before turning to Sam in question.

He tilted her chin up with two fingers and studied her face. "You look tired."

She shrugged, self-conscious beneath his scrutiny. "I've slept better," she admitted. "I wasn't sure how this would go down with her." She didn't see any need to add that her concerns about her tenuous relationship with him had caused her more restless hours than the assignment had.

"Is she going to help us?"

"She said she would."

Sam nodded. "Yeah. But will she do it?"

"Yes," Dallas said, suddenly certain. "She'll do it. I think she's glad to have an excuse to change her mind. She can blame it on us, if she wants, but deep down, it's what she's been looking for as her time drew closer."

"Still trying to turn her into a latent Girl Scout?" Sam asked, his voice laced with amusement.

His indulgence annoyed her. Dallas pulled her chin out of his loose grasp and shook her head. "I know exactly what she is. But I like her, anyway. Her kid could end up with someone a hell of a lot worse." From personal experience, she could have recited plenty of examples. She didn't bother.

"Okay, so maybe you were right about her. Maybe she'll make it."

"Some do."

"I know. Not very many, but a few."

Dallas wiped her palms nervously against the legs of her jeans. "I'd better get out there. Polly will be getting restless."

"Hold on a minute, okay? There's something I wanted to tell you."

She watched as he ran a finger around the open collar of his white oxford shirt, wondering why he suddenly looked rather nervous. Her stomach tightened beneath the harness. "What is it?" she asked, her voice sounding strained in her ears.

Sam was watching her as closely as she studied him, making her all the more certain that what he had to say was important to them on a personal level. "Brashear called me in this morning. Said he has some good news for me."

When he paused, Dallas motioned impatiently. "What good news?" she prodded.

"I've been offered a promotion. Head of the homicide division in the Fifth Precinct. Brashear said it was a hell of a coup at my age. Said I should be proud."

Dallas's throat tightened to match her stomach. "He's right," she managed. "You should be very proud. What did you say to him?"

"Told him I'd think about it."

She knotted her hands in the hem of her loose shirt. "And have you been thinking about it?"

He ran a hand through his hair and nodded. "Yeah. Sure. Of course, I've only had a few hours...."

"And?"

He shrugged.

Dallas heartily regretted Sam's timing in bringing this up now, with Polly waiting impatiently for her. This was definitely something they needed to discuss in depth . . . but there just wasn't time. Or maybe, she thought with a sudden, sinking feeling, Sam didn't intend to discuss it with her. It was his decision to make, not hers. They certainly didn't have any real commitment.

"When are you planning to give an answer?" she asked.

He shrugged again. "I don't know. I told Brashear I want to get this case out of the way before I make any decisions."

Again, no mention of discussing it with her first. So why had he told her about it now if he didn't want her opinion? But then, she'd never been the type to wait for an invitation before expressing her opinion—especially not when it mattered this much. "It's not what you want, Sam," she couldn't resist telling him.

He avoided her eyes. "Maybe it is," he disagreed. "It would be a change of pace, a desk job, a significant pay raise."

"It's not what you want."

He shot her an impatient look in response to her repetition. "You can't know that. Even *I* don't know what I want these days."

"I do." She gestured around the examining room in which they stood, indicating the exam table, the shelves of medical supplies, the complicated equipment that had so intrigued Sam when she and Polly had entered. "This is what you want. It's what you've always wanted."

The flash of old, painful hunger appeared and vanished so quickly from his eyes that Dallas almost missed it. There was no expression at all on his face when he answered. "We've already talked about that. It's too late now. I'd be an idiot to chuck a good career, a guaranteed future, to go chasing after some dream I had when I was just a green kid."

"You'd be an idiot to give up your dreams just because you're scared to go after them," Dallas retorted with her usual tact and delicacy.

Sam scowled, and Dallas wished she'd expressed herself a bit differently. But, damn it, it made her so mad when anyone just gave up on their dreams without a fight. Had *she* done so, she'd be right out there on those streets beside all those Pollys who hadn't believed they had any other choices.

"I don't remember asking for your advice," Sam said coolly.

Even though she knew he was worried, knew he was dealing with his own insecurities, his own pain, his words still hurt her. She managed a curt nod. "You're right, of course. This is none of my business."

"Damn it." He reached out to her, his expression a mixture of regret and annoyance. "Dallas—"

She evaded his touch by stepping back toward the door. "I've got to go. Polly won't wait long, and she and I really should go back together."

"Look, Dallas, I . . ."

Her hand was already on the doorknob. "We have a job to do, Sam," she reminded him unnecessarily. "I have to get back to it."

His hand fell to his side. "I know."

She opened the door.

Sam caught her shoulder before she could step out into the hallway. "Take care of yourself," he murmured. "Don't do anything stupid, you hear?"

"Telling me how to do my job again, Perry?" she asked, her bruised ego still smarting.

He forced a smile. "Telling you that I care what happens to you," he corrected.

There didn't seem to be anything she could say to that. Her eyes burning, Dallas nodded, hitched the harness more comfortably against her stomach, and walked away from him.

12

TWO NIGHTS LATER, Dallas was brought out of a sound sleep by a heavy pounding on her apartment door. Disoriented, she groped for the light, swore when she knocked the clock to the floor, then swung her legs over the edge of the bed. The pounding grew louder.

"Dallas! Dallas, hurry up!"

The voice was Polly's. Dallas snatched up the harness and stuffed it under her nightshirt, fastening only enough straps to keep it temporarily in place as she bolted for the door. Polly had been generally avoiding her for the past two days, still hurt and angry that Dallas had lied to her. There was only one reason Dallas could imagine that Polly was seeking her out now.

She jerked open the door. Polly stood in the hallway, gasping, her face pale without its usual coating of cosmetics, her dark hair limp around her shoulders. She was wearing an oversize satin nightgown. The front of it was soaked with a dark liquid.

"Your water broke?" Dallas asked, glancing down.

Polly nodded, one hand pressed against her stomach. "I'm in labor. God, it hurts."

Dallas drew the woman inside the apartment. "How far apart are the pains?"

"I don't know. Not—" Polly winced and nearly doubled over with the force of a contraction. "Not very far," she said when she could speak again.

"I'll get some clothes on. Have you called anyone? A cab? An ambulance?" She knew Polly didn't have a telephone, either, but she had to ask. Maybe she'd used the pay phone down in the lobby.

Polly shook her head. "I got rattled," she admitted. "I couldn't think what to do. This wasn't supposed to happen for another week or two."

"I know. Hold on just a second, I'll be right back." Dallas sprinted for the bedroom. She threw on the blouse and jeans she'd worn earlier, slid her feet into a pair of loafers and ran her fingers through her hair, wishing she had a phone.

Less than five minutes had passed when she rejoined Polly. Dallas was appalled to find Polly writhing in the grip of another contraction. "Oh, hell," she murmured. "They *are* close, aren't they?"

Polly only nodded, her lips tightly compressed.

Dallas had been trained in first aid, knew the rudiments of delivering a baby if she had to. She very much hoped she wouldn't have to. Her movements swift and efficient, voice brusque and bracing, she helped Polly remove the drenched nightgown and replace it with an oversize nightshirt of Dallas's. The garment usually hung on Dallas; it barely stretched over Polly's swollen stomach. Then Dallas wrapped her in a blanket from her bed and hustled her toward the door. "Okay, let's go," she said. "We'll try to get a cab downstairs."

She would have liked to call Sam to come after them, but regardless of the circumstances, she had to keep their cover in mind. To anyone watching, Dallas was no more than Polly's pregnant friend, offering support and assistance in Polly's time of need.

They made it to the hospital with little time to spare. A harried nurse announced that Polly was already fully dilated and the baby had dropped into position. "You the coach?" the nurse asked Dallas, glancing downward at Dallas's bulging middle. "If so, you're going to have to wash up and try to get into a scrub suit."

"Oh, I'm not—"

"Yes!" Polly gasped, reaching out to clutch Dallas's arm. She looked younger and more vulnerable without her armor of makeup and hairspray. And she looked scared. "She's my coach," she told the nurse. She looked up at Dallas from the wheelchair in which someone had stashed her. "Go in with me. You owe me this," she added quietly.

Dallas nodded. "All right. I'll wash up."

POLLY'S DAUGHTER ARRIVED less than an hour later—a fast, startlingly smooth delivery. The baby was wrinkled, gooey and loud in her protests at her abrupt change in surroundings. Looking at the tiny, disgruntled face surrounded by a mop of wet, dark curls, Dallas thought she'd never seen anything more beautiful in her life.

A nurse with a smile in her eyes carefully deposited the minute bundle into Polly's arms. Sweaty, exhausted and still dazed, Polly looked down at her daughter, and then up at Dallas. Her dark eyes were filled with tears, for the first time since Dallas had known her. "She really is pretty, isn't she?" Polly asked, her voice hoarse.

Dallas had to swallow hard before she could answer. "She's beautiful, Polly. She looks very much like you."

"Yeah. She sort of does, doesn't she?" Polly looked back down again, and laughed softly when the baby threw out a tiny hand and clipped her mother neatly across the chin.

IT WAS NEARLY THREE in the morning when Dallas dialed Sam's number from an isolated telephone in a conveniently deserted waiting room. His voice was gruff when he answered after three rings. She could picture him so clearly—his eyes heavy with sleep, his hair tousled, his chest bare above the gym shorts he favored for sleeping. She closed her eyes and savored the image, which had kept her company for the past two lonely days—and nights. "It's me," she said.

He sounded instantly more alert. "What's wrong?"

"Nothing. I just wanted to let you know that Polly had her baby. A girl. I was with her when it was born."

"You delivered it?" he asked, sounding startled.

She smiled and shook her head, as though he could see her. "No. We made it to the hospital. I was her coach. She had it so quickly that there wasn't time to give her any painkillers. She had to deliver naturally. She did great. Hardly even groaned, though I could tell it hurt like hell."

"Polly's tough," Sam reminded her.

Dallas thought of the softness on Polly's face when she'd looked down at her child. "In some ways," she agreed.

"A girl, huh?"

"Yes, and she's perfect. All her fingers and toes. A headful of hair. She's beautiful."

"Blivens will like that."

Dallas almost shuddered at the unpleasant reminder. "Yeah."

"You think Polly's going to keep the kid? Once we have the brokers in custody, I mean."

"I think so. I think she fell in love the minute they put the baby in her arms. I think it's the first time she's loved anyone in a very long time."

"Might be better for her to give it up. Legally," he added. "What kind of mother will she make, being a hooker?"

"A *former* hooker," Dallas reminded him a bit defensively. "She wouldn't be the first to successfully turn her life around."

"She'd be one of a very few," he countered.

Dallas shrugged. "There's always a chance."

Sam sighed heavily through the phone line. "Always the optimist."

"And you're always a pessimist. So maybe the truth lies somewhere in between."

"Yeah. Maybe." He paused a moment, then commented, "You sound dead on your feet. Tired?"

"Very," she admitted, rubbing wearily at the back of her neck. "But I wanted to let you know what had happened before I head back to the apartment."

"I'm glad you did."

There was a brief silence before Sam spoke again. "I don't like you being out alone at this hour. Want me to pick you up and give you a ride back to the apartment?"

Dallas shook her head, then remembered to verbalize the gesture. "No. Too risky."

"But—"

"I'm used to being on the streets at all hours, Sam. I'm a cop, remember?" she asked pointedly.

"Yeah," he said flatly. "I remember."

She didn't reply. She couldn't think of anything to say.

"Be careful," Sam said after a moment.

"I will," she promised.

He detained her just as she was about to disconnect the call. "Uh, Dallas?"

"What?"

"This is something else I couldn't plan—if I went back to school, I mean," he said, stumbling a bit.

She frowned. "What are you talking about?"

He cleared his throat. "Babies. Family. It would be several years before I'd be in any position to—well, you know."

Her cheeks warmed. "I—uh—didn't know you were planning to start a family anytime soon," she said, trying to sound offhand about it.

"I wasn't," he assured her hastily. "I just— It was just something that crossed my mind," he added, sounding uncharacteristically awkward.

"Oh. Well, lots of people these days are waiting to have families," she said, twisting the telephone cord around her finger. "Getting their careers established first. I've always figured I've got another fifteen years or so left for that sort of thing, myself. Not that we were talking about me, of course," she added hastily, thoroughly relieved that he couldn't see her flaming cheeks.

Sam didn't seem to notice her embarrassment as he doggedly continued. "What I mean is, it's ridiculous to even think about putting my life on hold to go back to school at this point."

Dallas was beginning to wonder which of them he was working hardest to convince—her, or himself. "It's ridiculous to throw your life away doing something you don't want to be doing," she argued.

He muttered something unintelligible. After another pause, he said, "This is a really stupid time to discuss this. The middle of the night, over the phone— I don't know what made me bring it up again."

Dallas suspected that the subject hadn't been off his mind since he'd been offered the promotion. It was eating at him. He felt torn between taking that bold risk and pursuing his old dream, or staying on the more secure path of the career he'd already carved out.

She wasn't without sympathy for him over his quandary, but she had seen the look in his eyes when he'd talked about his former plans. Sam would never be truly fulfilled, completely happy, as long as he stayed in a career he'd never wanted. His dissatisfaction was more than the usual burnout, more than a promotion and an increase in salary could remedy. His was a soul-deep disappointment that would always be there, would always haunt him with "what might have been."

How long would it be before his discontentment and her impatience drove them apart?

"You're right," she said finally, one hand pressed to her aching back. "This is a lousy time to discuss this. You're going to have to make your own decisions, Sam. You know what my opinion is."

"It's not that I don't value your opinion, Dallas."

She lifted her hand to her temple, which had started to ache along with her back and legs. She was tired and discouraged, painfully aware of a nagging little I-told-you-so voice inside her head—a voice that had warned her all along against becoming involved with Sam Perry. Hadn't she always known that they were just too different? That they were ill-matched as partners, much less as lovers. "I've got to go, Sam. I'm really tired," she murmured.

"Yeah. Get some rest. We'll talk again soon."

Dallas hung up with a heavy heart. She wasn't looking forward to that next talk. What if she found herself unable to accept what he would say? Chances were that he would tell her he'd accepted the promotion.

She didn't know whether he hoped to continue their relationship, and she no longer knew how she felt about it, herself. She loved Sam, and she respected the accomplishments he'd made in a career that he felt had been thrust upon him. But she'd worked so hard to pursue her own dreams, had refused to let anything stand in her way. Could she continue to respect Sam if she always secretly believed he'd been afraid to do the same for himself?

BLIVENS WAS JUST LEAVING Polly's hospital room when Dallas returned that evening. Standing just outside Polly's door, the hard-faced landlady glanced down at Dallas's stomach. "When's yours due?"

"Another couple of weeks," Dallas replied. "How is Polly?"

Blivens shrugged. "Seems okay."

"The baby's beautiful, isn't she?"

Blivens shot Dallas a sharp look. "I guess."

"I'm sure Myra's pleased."

Scowling, Blivens looked quickly around. "Shut up," she muttered. "Not here."

Dallas looked suitably chastened. "Sorry. But tell Myra hello for me. I hope she can pay me a visit when my own baby gets here." She stressed the word *pay*.

Blivens, hardly rocket-scientist material, got the hint. Her squinty eyes lighted up with an avaricious gleam and she smiled down at Dallas's stomach. "I'll tell her you said so."

The woman's smile made Dallas want to go take a shower. She let herself into Polly's room with only a quick tap to announce her arrival.

She found Polly lying alone in the semiprivate room, the other bed vacant. Polly was staring at the wall, her expression bleak. A small bouquet of mixed flowers rested on the nightstand.

"Who brought the flowers?" Dallas asked, though Polly's expression had already given it away.

"Blivens," Polly confirmed. "She told me the baby's beautiful. She seemed very pleased about it."

"I'm sure she is," Dallas said grimly. A beautiful baby girl could bring big dollars from the right sources.

"She said she'll be seeing me again real soon. Right after the baby and me are released tomorrow. Told me to make sure I dress the baby in the outfit she gave me."

Dallas expressed her opinion of Blivens in a few choice words.

Polly managed a weak smile in response. "Yeah," she agreed fervently. "But—"

"But what, Polly?"

"I'm scared." The words were little more than a whisper.

Dallas couldn't help wondering when Polly had last admitted such a vulnerability to anyone. "Are you afraid that you'll be hurt, or are you worried about your baby?"

"Both," Polly admitted. "But mostly I'm worried about the baby. She's so little . . . so helpless."

"But she's not alone," Dallas reminded her. "She's got you to protect her. And me, and Sam, and our fellow officers. Our first priority is that baby's safety, Polly."

"Your first priority is the bust," Polly muttered, looking away.

"No," Dallas said firmly. "It's not."

When Polly didn't immediately respond, Dallas spoke again. "You really think I could deliberately endanger that beautiful little girl, especially after I helped bring her into this world?"

Polly risked a glance back at her. "Well . . ."

"Just this once, let yourself trust someone," Dallas said. "I'm telling you the truth."

"It makes a nice change," Polly retorted, shooting a look at the harness Dallas wore.

Dallas didn't take offense. She figured Polly deserved the occasional shot.

In a very low voice, Polly gave Dallas all the details that Blivins had just given her. The "exchange" was to take place immediately after Polly and the baby left the hospital the next morning. The buyers wanted the baby as young as possible, Polly added bitterly.

Polly had been given the address of an abandoned warehouse in the city's old industrial district. She was to go there straight from the hospital, where she'd be met by Myra and Blivens. Blivens would bring along a couple of suitcases of Polly's things from her apartment. Myra would furnish the promised cash and a bus ticket to Michigan. Blivens would drive her to the bus station.

They wanted Polly to voluntarily disappear immediately after the exchange was completed.

"I asked if you could come with me," she added, twisting the bedsheet with nervous fingers. "I said it would help convince you to deal with them if they could see how easy the whole thing was for me. Blivens said no. They don't want any spectators, she said."

"Any witnesses, she meant."

"Yeah."

Dallas patted Polly's restless hand. "Don't worry. She won't see me immediately, but I'll be there. So will Sam. And a few others to give us a hand."

"I don't like taking the baby into that situation," Polly fretted.

"It's the safest place for her," Dallas reasoned. "She'll have cops all around to watch out for her. But try to run with her, and Myra and her boyfriend will track you down. Who'll protect your baby then?"

Polly sighed. "Even you can't believe that taking the baby into that warehouse is the safest place for her."

Dallas had to concede the point. "Okay, so it would be better if you were taking her home. But, under the circumstances, she'll be better guarded there than anywhere else."

This time it was Polly who conceded. "All right. But if anything happens to my baby..."

It wasn't necessary for her to complete the threat. Dallas nodded to acknowledge that she'd gotten the message. "We'll take care of her, Polly. By the way, have you thought of a name for her? It seems odd to keep calling her 'the baby.'"

Polly's eyes lighted up. "I read this book once—when I was a kid, you know? It was about these four sisters, and the oldest one wanted to be a writer."

"*Little Women?*" Dallas guessed.

"Yeah, that was it. Did you read it, too?"

Dallas nodded gravely. "It's a wonderful book. Do you want to name your baby Jo?"

Polly shook her head. "Amy," she said. "That was my favorite sister. I always said if I ever had me a little girl, I'd name her Amy."

Dallas couldn't stifle her smile. Of course, Polly's favorite character had been the vain, unabashedly materialistic sister. "I think Amy's a beautiful name," she said.

"Yeah. Me too." Polly looked up expectantly when a uniformed nurse wheeled in a clear plastic crib. "Looks like it's bottle time."

The nurse grinned. "Sure is. And your daughter's been letting us hear about it."

"That's my kid," Polly said proudly, even as little Amy wound up for another piercing shriek.

Dallas didn't linger much longer. She had a great deal to do, and little time in which to do it if Polly and Amy were to be safe.

DALLAS WAS UTTERLY delighted to be the first officer to step out of the deep shadows of the warehouse the next day. She held her badge in one hand, a weapon in the other. And she was smiling with the cold satisfaction of knowing her assignment was nearing a successful completion.

Four adults stood in one corner of the massive room—Polly, holding her baby and looking very

nervous, Ms. Blivens, Myra, and Myra's beefy boyfriend, Burt. Myra had just handed Polly a small vinyl
case and was reaching for the baby. That was all Dallas
had been waiting for.

"Take the baby and step back out of the way, Polly,"
Dallas ordered. "The rest of you stay where you are.
You're under arrest."

Myra, Burt and Blivens whirled in response to Dallas's voice. Burt took an instinctive, threatening step
toward her.

Sam came out from behind a pile of clutter behind
them. "Freeze." He, too, held a weapon, and it was
trained unerringly on Burt's chest.

Two uniformed officers appeared from outside. One
of them escorted Polly and the baby safely out of the
warehouse. The other moved to assist Dallas and Sam.

Burt cursed, threatening Sam with charges of false
arrest and entrapment. Blivens was wringing her hands
and loudly bewailing her innocence. "I ain't done
nothing wrong," she insisted. "You can't prove nothing."

"Quiet," Myra hissed to them both, looking harried.

Dallas knew Myra was well aware that Blivens would
tell everything she knew at the first hint of a plea bar-
gain. Myra was the only one of the three smart enough
to know just how bad the situation really was.

Dallas decided it would be a pleasure to take care of
this one, herself. She took a step closer to Myra. "You
have the right to remain silent," she began.

Myra gave her a withering look, taking in every detail of Dallas's slender body. Dallas had been delighted

to leave the harness off for this confrontation. "I know my rights."

"And you know that I'm going to read them to you, anyway," Dallas replied. This bust was going strictly by the book. No clever attorney would get these three off on technicalities.

Blivens gave an outraged squeal when the uniformed officer placed a hand on her shoulder to escort her out. "Get your hands off me!" she shrieked. "I ain't done nothing wrong, I tell you. You can't arrest me."

Burt jerked when Sam turned toward him. "I'll walk out on my own," he snarled, then promptly stumbled over a broken wooden crate behind him. He fell heavily, all two hundred and fifty pounds of him slamming into Dallas's left leg. She staggered, trying to right herself.

Blivens screamed and made a dash for the exit. The uniformed officer moved to intercede. Sam bent warily toward Burt, plastic manacles in hand.

While the other two officers were occupied, Myra proved that she was every bit as sharp and quick as Dallas had suspected. Without the slightest hesitation, she snatched up a solid piece of the broken crate and brought it down on Dallas's right arm before Dallas had even regained her balance from Burt's accidental tackle. Dallas cried out at the sharp crack of the blow. The gun fell from her suddenly nerveless fingers.

Dazed from pain, she found herself held tightly against Myra's wiry body almost before she realized it, her own gun pressed to her temple. *Damn*, Dallas thought, sickly suspecting that her arm was broken. *Something like this always happens when I work with Sam.*

"Don't move," Myra said when Sam edged instinctively toward Dallas. Myra pressed the gun more tightly against Dallas's temple.

"Myra, you can't get away with this. Why are you making this harder on yourself?" Dallas gasped, her stomach churning at the pain still radiating from her right forearm.

"Just shut up, okay? I have to think."

Sam's hands were spread in a nonthreatening stance, his gun held loosely in his right hand. "Let her go," he said quietly, his eyes never leaving Myra's face. Watching him, Dallas saw the rigidity of his jaw, the slight twitch of a muscle in his cheek. Had it not been for those faint signs, she would have thought him perfectly calm. She knew he was anything but.

"Don't be stupid, Myra," Blivens snapped, from her position behind the uniformed officer who'd returned from escorting Polly out just in time to get caught up in the tense situation. "You're only going to make it worse for all of us."

"She's right, Myra," Burt said glumly, still sitting on the floor where he'd fallen, the other uniformed officer's gun trained steadily on him. "Give it up."

"Shut up!" Myra retorted. "Both of you. I'm not going to jail. I can't go to jail."

"You have no choice," Sam said.

Dallas felt Myra tense and knew the woman was close to panic. Panic and handguns were a truly lousy combination, she thought glumly, waiting impatiently for the first opportunity to take action. If only her arm didn't hurt so damned much.

Myra took a step backward, pulling Dallas with her. "We're going to walk out of here," she said. "Just the two of us. The rest of you stay right where you are and she won't get hurt."

There was dead silence in the warehouse as Myra took another step backward and then another. Dallas heard the woman's breathing just behind her ear, sharp and uneven. The panic was growing. Dallas could only hope the fear would make Myra grow careless. Both she and Sam were poised to take advantage of the first opening.

Myra stepped on something small and round, momentarily lost her footing. She recovered quickly, but Dallas was already in motion. She spun and kicked out. Myra dodged the kick and leveled the weapon. Sam leapt forward.

A shot reverberated through the huge building, echoing through Blivens's screams and the shouts of the officers. Sam hit Dallas with all his strength, sending her flying. She landed on her injured right arm. An explosion of pain shot through her, nearly driving her straight into unconsciousness. She curled into a ball, gagging and cradling her arm against her stomach.

She no longer had any doubt that the arm was broken.

Concentrating on staying conscious and fighting down nausea, she was hardly aware of the pandemonium around her. She heard excited voices, angry shouts. The wail of sirens grew steadily louder—someone had called for backup. She spared a moment to think of Polly and the baby. She knew they were safe. She hoped Polly wasn't frightened.

Damn, but her arm hurt. Just wait until she had a chance to talk to Sam about his totally unnecessary flying tackle.

She opened her eyes after a few moments to find one of the uniforms kneeling beside her. "You okay?" he asked urgently, his hand on her shoulder. "Were you hit?"

"My arm is broken," she managed, knowing she must look like death. "Is everything under control?"

"Yeah. We've cuffed all three of them and called for an ambulance."

Dallas drew in a deep breath, trying to settle her stomach. It didn't help that the warehouse smelled so bad. "I really don't need an ambulance," she said, momentarily closing her eyes against a fresh wave of pain. "It's just a broken arm."

"It wouldn't hurt you to ride in an ambulance. And besides, we need it for Sam."

Dallas's eyes flew open. "Sam?"

Where the hell *was* Sam? She'd assumed he was helping subdue Myra and the others. But—an ambulance? "What's wrong with Sam?"

"He's been hit. Took one in the shoulder."

"Oh, my God." Dallas was already struggling to her feet. She swayed as blood rushed from her head with her movement.

"Hey, careful! Take it easy. He's going to be okay."

She ignored the officer who was frantically steadying her. She could see Sam now, lying on the floor on his back, another uniformed officer leaning over him while two others escorted their sullen prisoners out of the warehouse. She made it to his side and knelt quickly beside him, fighting the dizziness her rapid movements cost her. "Sam? *Sam!*"

His face was colorless and there was blood on his shirt. A lot of blood. The officer beside him held something tightly against the wound.

Sam opened his eyes in response to Dallas's voice. "Hey, Sanders," he said, his voice pathetically weak. "You okay?"

"I'm fine. Damn it, Perry, you just had to do it again, didn't you? I had everything under control. I didn't need you charging in to rescue me!" Her fear for him made her voice sharp. Her eyes burned; she blinked rapidly to clear them.

He managed a weak smile. "I know. The Lone Ranger on steroids."

"Exactly. I can handle my job, Perry. I don't need you taking care of me."

"Yeah, I know, but I can't seem to stop. I guess it's a good thing we won't be working together again, huh?"

"What does that mean?" she asked, brushing aside the officer who was trying to steady her as she swayed on her knees.

"I really hate this job," he muttered, his eyes closing again. "Always have. Looks like it's time to try something different."

She swallowed and touched his too-pale cheek, uncertain whether he was talking about the promotion or medical school. Right now, she didn't really care. "Yeah," she said huskily. "You'd better do it while you're still basically in one piece."

"Basically."

"The ambulance is here," someone said from close behind Dallas. "C'mon, Sanders, let someone take a look at that arm for you. We've got to clear the way for the paramedics to get to Perry."

Dallas nodded. "The paramedics are here, Sam," she said, in case he hadn't heard. "I'll be close by, okay?"

"Yeah." He opened his eyes just as a man and a woman in matching blue jumpsuits rushed to his side. "Hey, Sanders?"

"What is it, Sam?"

"I love you."

Aware of the speculative looks that had suddenly turned her way from several different directions, Dallas kept her gaze firmly on Sam's face. "I love you, too."

He smiled faintly and closed his eyes. "We're naming the first kid Bob," he murmured. And lapsed into unconsciousness.

Dallas promptly burst into tears.

Epilogue

IT WAS LATE, AFTER ten at night. His arms loaded with heavy textbooks, Sam trudged down the still-hot sidewalk toward his apartment building. He'd just spent a long evening at the university library. His eyes burned, his head and shoulders ached, and he was hungry. He couldn't wait to get home.

A young person in a battered baseball cap, a torn, sleeveless sweatshirt and grubby jeans loitered in the shadows just outside Sam's building. Looked like a restless teenager itching to get into trouble, Sam thought, with a sigh of resignation.

"Psst. Hey, mister. You look kinda tired. Got something here that will perk you right up," the shadowy figure hissed, reaching furtively into a pocket of the baggy jeans. "You interested in making a deal?"

Sam paused. "How much you asking?"

"It's expensive stuff," he was gravely assured.

"I'm kind of strapped for money right now," he explained. "I'm in medical school, you know. Got a mountain of student loans to pay off eventually. Would you consider giving me credit?"

Dallas tipped her baseball hat upward with one thumb, allowing the streetlight to illuminate her unpainted face. With her hair in a scraggly ponytail and a smudge of dirt on one cheek, she looked exactly like the young troublemaker she'd been pretending to be for the past week for an undercover campus drug investigation.

"Credit, huh?" She eyed him speculatively. "Got any collateral?"

He glanced down at his left hand. "Only this gold ring."

She pulled a thin chain from beneath her sweatshirt, displaying the ring that hung from it. "I've already got one just like that," she told him.

"Well, I guess that only leaves my body."

"Hmm," she murmured, slowly circling him. "It's not a bad body. I might consider it."

He grinned and swatted her shoulder. "You should consider yourself lucky to have a shot at it."

"Oh, I do," she assured him. "Damned lucky." And then she rose on tiptoe and kissed him. "Welcome home, Sam."

Oblivious to their surroundings, Sam kissed her thoroughly before drawing reluctantly away. He always greeted her with hidden relief that she had made it home unscathed again. He would always worry about her, would always chafe against the dangers of her job; but he knew she was doing exactly what she wanted to do. Just as he was.

Her salary, his disability pay and a student loan that would one day have to be repaid were putting him through medical school. He was in his second year now, and it would be some time yet before they had any money to spare. Neither of them ever complained. They were both pursuing careers they loved. And they were together.

They made a great team. They worked together to keep the apartment clean. They liked the same movies and music, and both enjoyed Dallas's cooking. They argued frequently, of course—they still couldn't agree on a name for the child they were planning to have as soon as finances allowed, for example—but they made up spectacularly.

Dallas smiled up at him, her brilliant eyes glowing in the artificial light. "About that pick-me-up I'm offering . . ."

Sam quirked an eyebrow. "I'm interested," he assured her.

She looped her arm through his, careful not to dislodge the mountain of textbooks. "It's not something I want to go flashing around the streets," she told him as they walked together toward the apartment. "I've got it well hidden. I'm afraid you're going to have to search me for it."

Sam chuckled. "I'm looking forward to it. But I warn you—it might take quite a while."

She hugged his arm. "We've got the rest of our lives," she said huskily, happily.

As he entered the building at his wife's side, Sam felt like the luckiest, richest man in the world.

Dallas had taught him how to dream again.

Do you have a secret fantasy?

Celebrity author and recluse Emma Jordan does. She is collaborating on a screenplay of her bestselling erotic thriller with talented, sexy-as-sin Sam Cooper. Once he's gone, she knows she'll never see him again. He'll be playing the starring role in their movie...just as he has been in her fantasies.... Experience the seduction in #526 *Obsession* (February 1995), by a fabulous new writer, Debra Carroll.

Everybody has a secret fantasy. And you'll find them all in Temptation's exciting new yearlong miniseries, **Secret Fantasies.** Beginning January 1995, one book each month focuses on the hero or heroine's innermost fantasy....

Take 4 bestselling love stories FREE

Plus get a FREE surprise gift!

MOVE OVER, MELROSE PLACE!

> Apartment for rent
> One bedroom
> Bachelor Arms
> 555-1234

Come live and love in L.A. with the tenants of Bachelor Arms. Enjoy a year's worth of wonderful love stories and meet colorful neighbors you'll bump into again and again.

First, we'll introduce you to Bachelor Arms' residents Josh, Tru and Garrett—three to-die-for and determined bachelor buddies—who do everything they can to avoid walking down the aisle. These three romantic comedies, written by bestselling author Kate Hoffmann, kick off this fabulous new continuity series from Temptation:

BACHELOR HUSBAND #525 (February 1995)
THE STRONG SILENT TYPE #529 (March 1995)
A HAPPILY UNMARRIED MAN #533 (April 1995)

Soon to move into Bachelor Arms are the heroes and heroines in books by our most popular authors—JoAnn Ross, Candace Schuler and Judith Arnold. You'll read a new book every month.

Don't miss the goings-on at Bachelor Arms

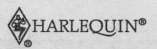

If you are looking for more titles by

GINA WILKINS

Don't miss these fabulous stories by one of
Harlequin's most distinguished authors:

Harlequin Temptation®

#25492	TAKING A CHANCE ON LIFE	$2.99	☐
#25500	DESIGNS ON LOVE	$2.99	☐
#25558	RAFE'S ISLAND	$2.99	☐
#25586	JUST HER LUCK	$2.99	☐
	(limited quantities available on certain titles)		

TOTAL AMOUNT	$
POSTAGE & HANDLING	$
($1.00 for one book, 50¢ for each additional)	
APPLICABLE TAXES*	$ _____
TOTAL PAYABLE	$ _____
(check or money order—please do not send cash)	

To order, complete this form and send it, along with a check or money order
for the total above, payable to Harlequin Books, to: **In the U.S.:** 3010 Walden
Avenue, P.O. Box 9047, Buffalo, NY 14269-9047; **In Canada:** P.O. Box 613,
Fort Erie, Ontario, L2A 5X3.

Name: _____

Address: _____ City: _____

State/Prov.: _____ Zip/Postal Code: _____

*New York residents remit applicable sales taxes.
 Canadian residents remit applicable GST and provincial taxes.   HGWBACK1